When the Bottom
Falls Out

and other stories

[signature] H Nigel Thomas

08/05/2015

We acknowledge the support of the Canada Council for the Arts for our publishing program. We also acknowledge support from the Government of Ontario through the Ontario Arts Council.

We acknowledge the financial support of the Government of Canada through the Canada Book Fund for our publishing activities.

  Canada

Cover design by Ingrid Paulson

Library and Archives Canada Cataloguing in Publication

Thomas, H. Nigel, 1947-, author
    When the bottom falls out : and other stories / H. Nigel Thomas.

ISBN 978-1-927494-40-0 (pbk.)

    I. Title.

PS8589.H4578W44 2014   C813'.54   C2014-903769-4

Printed and bound in Canada by Coach House Printing

TSAR Publications
P. O. Box 6996, Station A
Toronto, Ontario M5W 1X7
Canada

www.tsarbooks.com

For my aunt Elmena Dickson, 1910-2001

CONTENTS

Guilty and Innocent

"WHAT YOU MEAN, PASTOR?"

"Just like I says, Sister. I ain't committin' her to the ground."

Molly McClean stood on the porch of the recently built manse, so recent that the raw cement burned her nostrils. Her collapsed lips moved nervously. And her yellow rheumy eyes, deep in her narrow chocolate face, tried to focus on the brown earth. The yard still showed the scars where the debris from the recently constructed house had been removed. The red of the plaid kerchief round her head stood out prominently. She was a thin, short woman wearing a green shift. "Pastor Johnson, you ain't got no right to say you not burying she. You just come here from Kansas. You don't know a thing 'bout this woman."

"Sister McClean, I wants you to unnerstand one thang. I take ma orders from the Lord. And your Sister Roberta is a abomination unto the Lord. She done commit murder. And the Lord, He done tell me that she is a reprobate, to be cast in the pit on the last day. It ain't ma business, Sister, to be yoked with unbelievers. This er, Roberta, she been saved and sanctified 'cordin' to the Holy Scriptures?"

"I don' know, Pastor."

"Well, if she'd a been you'dda known, Sister. A light can't shine but a body see it, Sister. And I ain't doing no truck with unbelievers."

"Pastor, suppose I tell you a little bit of the story? Maybe you will understand. Everybody did think she wouldda hang. Let me tell you the story, Pastor."

He nodded, pointed to one of the two balcony chairs, and sat in the other.

"It start a dry weather season just like now. It musta been sometime in December or else January 'cause when we get to the shortcut where it all happen, it wasn't really that long since we did leave Brownie meeting, and that used to finish around half past five. When we get to the short cut, it been already dark and the moon bright. When we was half way up the stretch, we hear footsteps running away from we and through the banana field. And we come frighten 'cause ghosts used to be plenty them times. Anyway was four of us, so we continue walking. When we get where the bluff was high above the road and a little foot track go through the banana plantation down to the river, we see a man lying on the ground. We was afraid. Betsy Brown—God bless her, she done dead and gone—was the first one with the courage to approach the man. "O Gawd, is Bertie! Somebody done stab him. Come look. Blood pouring outta him. Milly and Patricia, go call help. Molly, let we stay here 'til they come back." That Betsy, give her that. She had brains. She later come a school teacher. Anyhow 'bout ten minutes later the people from the village start to come, and soon after that the police and the ambulance and everybody. Betsy say she think he did done dead; and sure, when the police come, they say they did think so too.

"Well, Pastor Johnson, that was the talk of this village for years 'cause is years the case take. Anyhow lemme come back to that right after. Well, the same night the police find a knife long like my arm sharpen two sides, and a half-nose man in the crowd say that she did buy the piece of steel from him and borrow his file and was working on it for two weeks.

"It really was the dry weather in truth 'cause when the police couldn' find her for 'bout five days, they was planning to set the canefields round the place on fire 'cause they was certain she hidin' in them. But they catch her just as they was 'bout to light them.

"Funny thing though, you know, is only 'bout five years ago, I find out the real story. Everybody know he used to beat her, that he cause her one time to lose a child; another time he say that she throw away one—'cause o' that she ain't got any friends here—but we going come back to that. Well, she used to get beat steady. But everybody know that wasn' a reason to take a life.

"Well Bertie, he was a champion steel band man. And they have the funeral on a Saturday. And everybody and all the steel bands from all over the country come. Oh it was a big funeral. When Father Flatelley finish with the sermon there wasn' a dry eye in the church. And it was the first time a steel band ever play in the church. Father Flatelley he say what a fine, handsome, upright man Bertie been. And 'cause we was sad we all agree. But now I think 'bout it, Pastor, that priest had to run away from here years later 'cause he use to interfere with the altar boys—he was a white man just like you, only thing his eyes wasn't blue, they was green—so if you put two and two together, you will see why he did find Bertie so nice, 'cause he and Bertie was good friends.

"Well, everybody say she work obeah on Bertie. Bertie mother tell everybody so. And we did all believe it. Bertie mother say Bertie couldn' leave her 'cause she give Bertie something to eat that tie

Bertie to her.

"Well, while all this was going on, there was a nice black woman here from America. She was organizing the maternity wing o' the hospital in Hanovertown. Her name was Olive Taylor. Plump, brown skin woman with a deep voice, and a smile like melting butter. Well, Olive went to the jail to see her. And Olive she organize to have her friends from America pay for the trial 'cause Olive tell the papers the way men treat women here—and we didn' have no women lawyers; we have some now—she ain't think no local lawyer wouldda put his heart into the trial, and if is government what paying the lawyer, well she know he ain't going do a good job. 'Sides she didn' know one that wasn' beating his wife, most o' them in private. And ain't that the gospel truth! Lawyer Cole knocked the sight clean out of his wife right eye; and the one what they call Penniston, his wife had to leave he and run away to America. She used to get blows too much. So Olive Taylor, she get money from America, and the lawyer come from England. Tall malatta man, straight like a coconut tree. Before the trial over half the village testify on behalf o' the accused and the other half on behalf o' the dead man. And I ain't think we did know what we was doing 'cause we did all want she to hang. You see, Pastor, you is new here. But the way we see it, it ain't got no forgiveness for murder. That is we unpardonable sin what the Bible talk 'bout. And even before she kill him, nobody did respect her seeing how she didn' bring a child to term. People like that we don' think they clean. And we wouldn't o'drink water from a glass they touch. But we not so severe now as before.

"Well, that lawyer from England. He was a malatta. When he finished, you couldn' find the other one for the words he did done wrap him up in. I never hear more 'whearases' in my life, and 'points', and 'howevers', enough to make a body dizzy. So the jury find that she wasn't guilty. The government appeal and the trial start over again and they get another judge, this time from England. And the judge from England say that she wasn' guilty either."

"Well, Sister, that was only man's judgment; the Lord gon find her guilty at the Last Judgment."

"Pastor, it so strange that it always happen in the dry season. I watch a car drive by here few minutes ago and all the dust it leave, and it remind me o' the dust the donkeys was kicking up the days they was looking for her. Funny thing, too, the two trials take place during the dry season. I know this because the first one was bad. I used to have to get up at five and walk a half mile to the big river to get my bath so I could catch the seven o'clock bus to go to town for the trial seeing as I was one o' the witnesses. All the water in the small river what closer did done dry up. And when the judge pass the verdict after the second trial, that was the same day the rainy season start. It was so heavy that it wash away a bridge. Come to think 'bout it, some preachers like yourself did say that God send the drought to warn us to make the right decision in the case. And when the bridge wash away, some say God was showing us he wasn' please with the decision what the white man judge from England make. To tell you the truth, Pastor, even though nobody was talking to her and she used to stay sort of locked-up like at her mother house, we was all relieved that the whole thing was over.

"Now, when you tell me you not committing her to the ground, I feel like if we start the trial over again; and Pastor, I don' think you have the right to 'cause God make the rain to fall on the just and on the unjust."

"Amen to that, Sister McClean, but I ain't none too certain 'bout the unjust; now ain't no rain is gonna be a-fallin' when they is a-burnin'. But puttin' aside the unjust, Sister, I want you to unnerstand one thang. I take ma orders from the Lord and you takes your orders from me."

"Pastor Johnson!"

"You ain't deaf now, Sister McClean. I SAYS YOU TAKES YOUR ORDERS FROM ME. The Bible says that woman is under the governance of man. Here we is, Sister. I'm the man and the Lord's anointed. Is you goin' to listen to the voice o' the Lord or not, Sister?"

Molly McClean looked at him. She had heard little pieces of that nonsense all her life—all that stupidness 'bout men this and men that . . . and the Lord say this and the Lord say that—that got lost between the food she damn well had to scrub people floors and hoe their garden and wash their clothes to find food for her five children, none of whose fathers supported them. Fred once in a while would bring two dollars for the last one, but it wasn' for the child, it was 'cause he did want to sleep with her. Deep down she felt tired about all this men this and the Lord that.

"You don' got the right to judge her, Pastor. And I don' care what the Bible says."

"If you talks like that, Sister, I gon' have to summon you 'fore the church board."

"Why not the throne o' God, Pastor?" and she left.

It was midday, and the sun was scorching. Her house was about a mile from the Evangelical Manse. It had been no effort getting to the manse. Now it was very tiresome to walk home. She would get there: one step at a time and soon you walk a mile.

Imagine, dead at seventy-nine. Roberta Beckles. She was twenty-one when she killed Bertie. My children was afraid of her. All the children was afraid of her. She just stayed in that house. We used to see her bringing water from the river and after that the standpipe after pipe water come to Hillsdale. Sometimes taking the bus to town. In the last years she take care of her mother, and when she die, she go on living at the house. One good thing, brothers and sisters away never let her down. This one send five dollars, that one ten, that one a parcel. She manage. But is when the village see how nice she take care of her mother Beverley that their hearts start softening towards her.

Molly remembered the day when things really start loosening up between them. Molly was keeping a granddaughter for her daughter what was in Aruba. Beverley had taken for the worse and seeing as how they used to be all Methodist, she went to see Beverley. And her granddaughter, who was 'bout two, took to Roberta and went into her arms, and Molly didn' know what to say. And every time they passed the gate, her granddaughter would pull her toward the yard and call "Therta." Then Molly had to go to Trinidad to see another daughter what was there illegal and there was some mix-up 'bout the child birth certificate and she couldn' carry her, and seein' that the child did like "Therta" so much, she left her with her for three months. And is so the friendship start up.

Matter o' fact the night the Evangelicals start their revival, Roberta and she was there. When the power of the Lord knock her down, Roberta did even bend down over her. Funny, Roberta used to go to the Evangelical Church, but she never join it, never get save, nothing. She just used to go; guess 'cause they was new and the Methodists did done wash their mouths on her so.

"Lawd, Molly, you not 'fraid fo' yo' granddaughter? Why you not staying away from that woman?"

"You, if you know what good fo' you, better stay outta my business." That is how she did have to handle them.

One day, after Beverley did done dead and Roberta was living alone in the house, Roberta come up the hill a little ways to where Molly lived. She did done get just like a ship, big up top and small below, just like her mother people. And she had the big cheek bones and brown skin and broad face and long hair 'cause they was mixed with Carib. A tall woman too. She had on a pleated grey skirt and a cream bodice. And she was barefoot. Just like she in front of she now. She sit down on the piece of wooden plank that form the step, and she say to Molly, "You have such a nice cool breeze up here, and you can see all the way to the sea. I uses to come up to this hill plenty when I was a girl. I uses to just like to watch the sea and dream 'bout travelling."

"Why you never did travel? You don' think it wouldda been better to leave all that past behind you? Start a new life somewhere where people don' know you? I always wonder why you did that to youself."

"Travel where, Molly? They's things you don't know, Molly, 'cause you ain't never take nobody life. Things that ain't got nothing to do with lawyers, with trials, and with juries."

"God know I had it in my thoughts many time to kill my last child father, but I ain't never had your courage."

"It ain't courage, Molly. It ain't that. It's something else. Lemme see. You see I was sixteen when I take up with Bertie and he been twenty. 'Bout six months after, I get pregnant, and one night he put *one* beating on me, I lose the baby. You know the story, 'cause Marjorie did meet me lying just where Bertie leave me, and I couldn't move, and she call help and move me, and she tell the court that at the trial. Well, you wouldn' believe what that beating was for, Molly. You probably didn' believe when you hear it in court. He use to like to have me both ways, but he always used to start the back way. I didn' like it, and he always used to punch me, and unless I groan for pain he wouldn' stop. So that night anyhow, I decide he wasn' going to have me that way, and I insist, and more he beat me more I insist, until he knock me down and kick me in the stomach. I think he did think I dead, 'cause I did pass out."

"What about the obeah part?"

"Obeah! What obeah? Me work obeah on him! To kill him, yes. To keep him, oh no! I not saying if he was a loving man and he did start to fool 'round with another woman, I wouldn't o' try a little something. But I never once enjoy sex with him, and I couldn' leave him."

"Don' talk nonsense."

She shake her head and she get up and she breathe in deep. "No Molly, *he* wouldn' leave me. There's plenty things we don' understand in this society. When I tell him we finish, he come and pull me outta my mother house and beat me, right in our yard. When I went to the police station. Big-gut Barrow was sergeant at the time. You know what that swell-gut tell me. 'What you come to complain on the man for?' Then, he ask me all kindsa questions 'bout what happen, but he ain't write nothing down. Then he tell me to go home and he going see 'bout it. Weeks past, and Bertie did done beat me two times since. I go back to him again. He say to me, Swell-gut say to me, 'I ain't make no case, 'cause your boyfriend say you done give him something to eat what tie you to him, and is when the something rise up in him that he does beat you. Don' come back here and waste we time. We is busy people."

"Well, as you know, we was very poor. Daddy did done stop writing us long time before that. We didn' know if he was dead or alive in Trinidad. But Ma was thinking 'bout trying for a lawyer. Round 'bout that time that scandal 'bout the civil servant woman and her husband was on the radio and in the papers. You remember the one? I can't remember her name now. But her husband used to beat her, and she hire a lawyer and sue him for abuse. The lawyer for the husband argue that under the law he could beat her with anything what wasn't bigger than his thumb. You don't remember that case?"

"It coming back to me now."

"Well, anyway the lawyer what represent the woman argue that he used to slap she and that his hand bigger than his thumb. And the judge agree and find the husband guilty. But the sentence was that the husband should go home and live peaceful with his wife. And the lawyer for husband ask the judge, 'If he hit her with something smaller than his thumb, that legal?' And the judge nod. That was the part that cause the scandal."

"Wait, wasn't that the same woman what put manchineel in her husband tea?"

"Same one. One week after the judge pass the sentence. You remember they didn' hang her 'cause she was 'from a good family'?"

"Yes, the whole thing coming back to me now. She was to spend she lifetime in jail. But they release her a few years ago, after fifteen years."

"That is why that woman from America try to help me 'cause I wasn' from no *good* family, and is hang they wouldda hang me.

"So Molly there wasn' anything I couldda do. I throw away the children. He know 'bout one, but is three I throw away. Bring *his* children into the world! I used to do it myself with a piece o' wire.

"I wouldn' tell you no lie, I did even think 'bout killing myself. One night I drink five aspirins, so I guess I really wasn' serious and I didn' try no more.

"One day I was just coming round the corner where he uses to sit under the gallery o' the rum shop and play cards, and I hear him carrying on 'bout how I does beg him to do it to me by the back door. Then he tell them how he does put me in all sort of position and how he doesn' stop until I bawl. The sonofabitch didn' know how true that was. Only I never used to bawl for him to hear, 'cause I did done suspect that is what he want. Some men is strange, Molly. Really strange."

"Don' tell me. Every last one run from me after they done breed me. The other one what used to hang around sometimes used to pretend he giving me money for the child when all he been doing is treating me for a whore, until I just tell him to wipe his arse with that two dollars. I know 'bout them, but your Bertie beat all."

"That is what decide me, Molly. That is what get me going. After that you wouldn' know how easy it come. I know he wouldda been coming from Camden that Friday, so I set out with the knife. I know that when he see me, he wouldda want to show off and beat me and then pull me in the banana field and use me. And is right so it start to happen. Nobody was with him, and the long stretch did done get dark. So when he bend down to push his hand under my dress I pull the knife out from my frock sleeve—he ain't see it yet—and shove it in him.

"You know, the only thing I regret is that I did run and they take so long to find me."

Molly returned to the present as she came alongside the croton hedge separating the property of the Methodist Manse from the road. The minister was in. No problem, he told her, he would take the funeral.

Nehemiah Johnson, you ain't hear the last of me yet. I ain't one to be under no man "governance," like you say. When I finish with you, you will find yourself back in Kansas. You won't even have time to read me out o' the church that my few coppers help to build. Nehemiah Johnson. Governance. The gall!

Glimpses Into the Higginsons' Closet

A CLUMP OF BANANAS with as many as twenty large plants in the root grew by the side of the grey stone wall that separated the Higginson property from the stream that flowed a few metres below. A bird had built its nest atop one of the banana shoots. Licia had peered into the nest that was exposed to the sun and had seen three eggs in it. Sometimes the mother bird sat on the eggs and kept them warm. Every day Licia looked at them: she wanted to see how the eggs hatched. And she would not kill the baby birds like Patsy had done. It had made her flesh crawl to see it. Patsy had stomped that tiny bird—it looked so clean without any feathers—into a pulp, and they had all watched its tiny guts there on the gravel road. And Harriet had said that the spirit of the bird would choke Patsy. And the pipiri had shrieked whistles all around trying to find its young. That was really a bad thing Patsy did. No. She wouldn't kill them. She wanted to see them and touch their warm skin when their mother wasn't there. And she hoped their mother wouldn't come and find her there and try to pick her eyes out.

Near the banana clump was a pile of stones. They looked like an altar where animals were sacrificed, just like in the picture Licia saw in church. These stones had been left over from the construction materials that were used for the wing Mr Higginson had just added to his house. The stones provided an excellent perch for twelve-year-old Alicia. Everyone called her Licia, and she liked its hissing sound. Standing on the stones, Licia, in those rare moments when she managed to slip away from the chores of the Higginson household, would look across the stream at the two-room shacks there, at the community where her mother and father lived, in the shack that was closest to the Higginson property. They rented it.

From the stone pile she had watched her mother—"rawny-boned" and wiry—light up a fire of twigs she had gathered from the neighbouring fields, put her cast iron pot on the flame, and peel the tannias, green bananas, or breadfruit, whatever it was she had to prepare supper from. Licia had seen her mother cry often. She had seen her shaking hands, the same hands that had got her mother fired from one maid's job after another. But it was the swelling of her mother's stomach that intrigued Licia most. It occurred every time the grass was at its brownest and footsteps on the roads stirred up clouds of dust. Her mother would begin to groan and send her to go tell Brother Slater to go and get the midwife. Brother Slater would say, "Why is I have to go? Where Ansel is? I didn' breed you?"

Brother Slater knew where her father was. Everyone knew. Ansel spent his nights in a drunken stupor and his days sweeping, stacking, running errands for the owner of the rum shop so he could get his rum, and he would then stagger home and curse and sing and vomit in bed. Sometimes he drank the cheap Bay Rum, which people told him would shorten his life. Ansel was a Carib. He was different from his people, who lived isolated in a part of the island where the British had put them after banishing their leaders to a faraway country. She heard this from her uncles. Licia had seen how hard her uncles worked. They had barrels of salted meat and several bundles of dried fish in their houses. On evenings, after they had eaten, everybody gathered around in a large group, and the old men told stories about their brave deeds and the bad things white people had done them. Sometimes the men played the banjo and men and women danced a four-step dance they called the quadrille. Licia loved the week she had spent with them. But they did not like her father. They had told him he could come back to the community only when he had stopped drinking; they didn't want drunks in the family.

The midwife always took her time coming, for Rita owed her money for each of the babies she had delivered. Twice she'd arrived just in time to tie the baby's navel string. Once she didn't come at all. That time Licia was about eight. Her mother had asked her to go outside for a sharp knife and to light up a fire and put some water to heat on it. Licia had watched her mother cut the navel string and knot it and use the warm water to wash off the cornmeal-looking goo on the baby's body.

Licia knew what to expect thereafter. It meant that when the rains started, the baby's eyes would focus inward as if it wanted to see its nose, and instead of getting heavier the baby got lighter. It meant that her mother would spend hours slapping and kneading her breasts; it meant that Licia had to go to the fields in search of certain leaves, that were gathered at full moon when they were most powerful, to make tea for her mother, that would bring back her milk, but it never did. There would be a few trips to the clinic, bottles of bad-smelling medicine, and, after that, the baby's death. Her mother would then buy a codfish crate, two flour sacks, and a pint of rum. Brother Percy would make the baby's coffin from the crate; her mother would tear the flour sacks into strips; and the little children, dressed in white, if they possessed white clothes, or any colour, would gather at the shack. The coffin would be placed on the strips, and four children would lift it, holding the strips, and transport it across the stream, around the road by the school yard, past the cinema house, to the cemetery. The tiny coffin was marked *NEW FOUND 100 POUNDS COD FISH* in blue. Throughout the procession they sang, "We are but little children weak / Nor born in any high estate . . ." Finally the little brother or sister would be laid in a very shallow grave. Her mother would howl and say she wanted to be buried too. Sometimes her father was there, dry-eyed and already drunk. Licia cried too because it made her sad to see her mother cry.

For two years Licia had witnessed only the burials. Of course, from the pile of stones she had seen her mother's swelling stomach, then the flattening, and sometimes the infant nursing at her breast, and then one day– Licia usually had an idea when—Mrs Higginson would tell her she should go and see her mother, and Licia would know why. Today Licia looked across at her mother with the infant at her breast, the pot on the stones in the yard, and even the dust the wind raised.

At the other end of the yard, Mr Crowe, the gardener—a thin, light-skinned man, who limped and wore dungaree overalls—was whistling and sloshing whitewash on the long low wall that separated the flower beds from the rest of the yard. There were two huge piles of manure that Mr Crowe had to spread onto the flower beds when he finished whitewashing the walls. Licia wished he would hurry up and do that and cut the dead flowers because otherwise Mrs Higginson would shout at him, and Licia did not like the way he kept grinding his teeth afterwards for the rest of the day.

It was May, and Miss Connie, the only child of the Higginsons, was home from university. Licia frequently overheard Mrs Higginson talking to her friends about Miss Connie's studies. She was a student of classics at Manchester University. She returned home each May and left in September to return again in mid-December and leave again at the beginning of January. And Licia did not like that. Miss Connie had a way of remaining in her bedroom all day, and she would come to the window and shout at Licia if her Ovaltine had not been brought up or if it had not been cold enough. Then again at breakfast Miss Connie had a way of curling her lips and looking over her glasses and saying, "Licia, did you intend this oatmeal for me or for the pigs? Take it away. I'll have Corn Flakes instead." And if Mrs Higginson was near to Licia it almost always meant an insult. There were the two bowls she had broken, and Mrs Higginson had said that the money for her next two dresses would be used to replace those bowls, and she had continued to wear her calico dress long after the red flowers had washed out and it had large rips, and Mrs Higginson had found scraps of fabric and shown her how to patch the rips.

One afternoon while Licia was drying the dishes before putting them away, Miss Connie announced to her mother that she had to leave in twenty minutes to go to a fitting at the dressmaker's.

"Whose ball are you wearing that one to, Connie?"

"The Ambroses's, Mama."

"Hm, Hm! Watch out for those Ambrose boys. That oldest one is like a wild stallion. He got Mary Mills's daughter in the family way."

"Well, Mama, what do you want me to do? Aren't you glad I go to these parties? Didn't you say you want me to find a white husband?"

"Or almost-white. But dear, these people are not of the elect. They drink and dance and smoke. And your honour, Connie dear. Aren't you concerned about your honour? It's the greatest gift for your husband on your wedding night. I was twenty-eight when I married your father, and I am sure he wouldn't have married me if he thought I had lost it."

Connie remained silent.

"Are there any coloured people at these parties?"

"Now, now, Mama, you know the only coloured people to enter those gates are the maid and the gardener."

"Well, things have changed so much. One never knows. Since Patsy Spence ran off with that ace of spades without a penny, all mothers worry that their daughters might do the same."

"But Mama, Daddy married you."

"And what do you mean by that? Well, let me tell you, my marriage to your father was a gift from God . . . Don't look at me like that! And I am not really black. A little dark-skinned, yes. One of my grandfathers was white. I always prayed to God to get a white husband, and you should too. You don't want to bring black children into this world, do you? Don't you know black people are cursed? I can show you where the Bible says so. I got your father for serving the Lord faithfully. He's a reward for my righteousness. I come from a blessed family. My father started each day with morning devotions. If he made ten cents on the land, one cent went to the Lord. In the hardest of times we were never hungry. God saw to it that we were not, for we never wasted and we were righteous. My father worked from sunup to sundown."

Miss Connie yawned.

"And we all had our little ways of supporting ourselves. I grew lettuce and carrots which I sold on Saturdays to the wealthier people. Your Uncle Edgar raised sheep, and your Uncle Clifford kept pigs. It was our money that bought the things we needed, our church clothes and clothes for special occasions. Oh yes, my father was a black man but he brought us up right, God-fearing, and thrifty. I remember one day I was washing and I left the soap soaking in the water, and he walked up to me, touched my arm, and pointed to the soap and said, "See that, 'Waste not, want not.' I was so ashamed.

"I know the fruits of righteousness, Constance. Look at my brothers. One is now the inspector of schools, the other is the headteacher of the largest elementary school on Isabella Island. I was already a senoir teacher at twenty-eight when I married your father."

"Wouldn't you have preferred to teach? Your life seems so dull. You know what my friends call this house? *The Morgue*! And they say it's on account of you."

"And I hope you don't encourage them. I wish you'd keep God-fearing company."

"I'm doing the best I can, Mama. They are the only *white* boys around, Mama."

"Well, you just be careful. Don't drink and scandalize your father's good name. I don't mind about myself, I am nothing. And if those boys get fresh, don't give in."

"Mama, you don't think you push this black-white thing too far? At Manchester everybody knows I'm black. And they love me for it. I don't hide it. I keep photographs of you and Daddy and I show them to my friends."

"Constance, I have never called anyone this before, but now I will tell you this: you are a fool! You don't have to go announcing your blackness to the world. It won't get you anywhere. When you were leaving for England I warned you. Don't you remember? I told you to tell them you had Italian parents."

"Well, Mama, as you know, I'm not as God-fearing as you, so I told them the truth."

There was a long silence. Finally Miss Connie said, "Mama, it's time I go for my fitting."

Licia remained quietly in the kitchen. Her classmates said lots about the Higginsons. Patsy, whose father was a lay preacher in the Methodist church and a school teacher, said that Mr Higginson had put three tins of bully beef on her father's grocery account; and when her father told him that neither he nor his wife ate bully beef, Mr Higginson had laughed, crossed it out, and said, "Anybody could make an honest mistake." And Doris had said to her one day, "Don' play with us 'cause Miss Higginson don' like us." And Mary and Milly had started singing,

Licia wear Miss Connie hand-me-down drawers
Licia wear Miss Connie hand-me-down drawers
Licia wear Miss Connie hand-me-down drawers
And old man Higginson underpants.

And all the other children had laughed, and Percy had said that she should lift up her dress and show them if it's true; and they had all laughed again, and when she had begun to walk away, they all began to sing the song again; and she had had to run to class to get away from them. And Mariette, whom Licia liked, and who sometimes gave her a bite from her mango or golden apple, had told her that her father said that Mr Higginson charged three times as much as the goods cost in Hanovertown and that everybody knew that Mr Higginson was a thief. And one of the women who worked at the Higginson store had told her father that Mr Higginson put ground corn in the coffee and soaked down the codfish so that it would weigh heavy. And her father was going to buy coffee from Mr Higginson and take it to town and have it tested. Her father didn't like Mr Higginson—"No way! Good-for-nothing trash robbing black people. One day black people will drive them outta Isabella Island." Licia hoped they'd drive out Mrs Higginson too.

Licia turned around to see Mrs Higginson staring at her.

"Well, since I've been looking at you, you could have dried three sets of dishes and you haven't touched a single plate."

Licia resumed drying the dishes and Mrs Higginson left the kitchen . . .

And Gloria, whose mother worked for Doctor Anderson, said that Mrs Anderson used to laugh at Mrs Higginson. "Marie," she would say, to Gloria's mother, "Can you imagine, Amelia uses bleaching cream on that child's skin? Isn't she more intelligent than that? It's that that's responsible for the rashes on Connie's face. I told the Doc to warn her that those creams contain arsenic." And Gloria said that Mrs Higginson's last maid had said that when Connie was little she begged her father one day to tell her mother not to put a clothespin on her nose at night. And Mr Higginson went to the window and called to Mrs Higginson in the garden and told her to cut out the clothespin nonsense. "Your nose is flat as a bread board and still I married you. Stop tampering with this child's nose." Gloria's mother had told the story to Mrs Anderson, and Mrs Anderson would say to Gloria's mother, "Marie, tell me the story about the clothespin;" and Gloria's mother would repeat the story, and Mrs Anderson always laughed. And the first time Doctor Anderson heard the story he laughed so hard, he knocked over his wine glass and dropped his fork on the floor.

Licia had also heard Mrs Higginson telling Connie that she should not be too close with her cousins. And when Connie had asked her why, she had replied, "Well, you don't want their dark skins to lessen your chances now, do you? Stay away from them for your own good."

Miss Connie's lace dresses and rows of high heel shoes that matched her many purses always intrigued Licia, and she liked to clean Miss Connie's room for that reason. On Sunday mornings when the three of them were about to get into the car to go to the Anglican church where they worshipped, Licia always made sure she was somewhere where she could get a good look at Miss Connie. Licia would go with them to the 7 PM service but she had to stay home on Sunday morning to prepare their breakfast, because Mrs Higginson had got rid of the maid a year after Licia's arrival.

Today, standing on the stones and looking across the water at her mother, Licia's mind went back to the time when she went to live with the Higginsons.

It was a Sunday, and Mrs Higginson had come to visit their next-door neighbour, Brother Charley, who was in his last days. Mrs Higginson always visited the sick and needy if they were regular worshippers at the Anglican Church. That Sunday when she had gone to visit Brother Charley, she had seen Licia in her patches sitting on the stones in the yard and eating from a calabash. Of course, she lived near enough to the family to see or hear the beatings Ansel frequently gave Rita; she knew of the annual buryings, for Rita was a baptized Anglican; and as the people's warden in the Anglican church, Mrs Higginson sometimes deputized for the priest; it was usually she who found a lay preacher to conduct the funerals of the nonelect, when the priest was too busy. Mrs Higginson had looked at Licia sitting on the stones and it occurred to her that the stale bread she sometimes fed to the chickens could feed Licia, and with a few calico dresses at a shilling a yard (shoes were out of the question), Licia would be better off. It would be a deal that would cost her nothing. Soon Connie would leave for university so really she wouldn't need a maid. She would train Licia to take up the slack and after a year or two let the maid go. Licia had heard Mrs Higginson relate various pieces of the story to the different women who came for tea.

"Licia, where are your parents?"

"They in the house."

"Ansel and Rita, can I speak with you?"

They had taken sometime coming out. Ansel was grinning like a pleased dog, showing a lone upper tooth.

They were pleased that Mrs Higginson wanted to take Licia off their hands. "Take her right now," Ansel told her.

Licia had been excited. Now she wouldn't be hungry; she would have lovely dresses and things and live in the big house across the river. She went that same evening. That night she slept in one of Mrs Higginson's old dresses on a cot arranged in the store room off the kitchen. The following morning after the family had finished breakfast Mrs Higginson gave Licia a half of a penny loaf, a tiny piece of fried fish that would not have weighed an ounce, and a small porcelain cup of tea with enough sugar to dilute the bitterness and enough milk to turn it muddy. The family had had oatmeal covered with milk, freshly squeezed orange juice, bread baked that same morning, and ham and eggs.

The shouts, the insults, they were as regular as the ticking of the clock.

"Put that down!"

"Don't let the milk boil over!" Pow (a slap)! "Can't you watch what you're doing?"

"You've burned the oatmeal. Miss Connie won't have that."

"You are dripping water on the floor!"

"Don't touch my plates with your wet hands!"

"You want to send me to the Pauper's Asylum?"

"Why is your dress so filthy?"

"Why did I have to involve myself with scum?"

"You are as sloppy and useless as your good-for-nothing mother."

Sometimes Licia wished she could put her hands over her ears and block out Mrs. Higginson's shrieking voice. Worst of all, one morning after the maid had finished making pancakes, Licia slipped one into her bosom. It began to burn her and Mrs Higginson came into the kitchen at the same time, so Licia couldn't move. Her dress was loose, for Mrs. Higginson had made both her dresses, and she'd allowed for Licia's growth. The pancake slipped down her waist, and she held it with an arm across her stomach.

"Why aren't you stirring the oats?"

Licia picked up the spoon and the pancake fell onto the kitchen floor. Mrs Higginson saw it all.

Licia tried to speak but couldn't. Mrs Higginson put down her teacup. With her left hand she pushed Licia towards a chair and leaned her over, and kept spanking her until she was breathless.

When Mrs Higginson stood up, the maid was shaking her head in protest. Mrs Higginson saw her and averted her gaze and said somewhat defensively, "They begin by stealing small and end up stealing big—a pancake today, a thousand dollars tomorrow. 'Train up a child in the way he ought to grow, and when he is old he will not depart from it.'"

"You finish, Mistress? Now is my turn for tell you something. If you give this child a proper meal, she wouldn' have for steal."

"Get out! Get out!" Her scream was followed by the thudding footsteps of an alarmed Mr Higginson running down the stairs. He was red-faced, out of breath, and partially dressed. "In God's name, Amelia! Are you having a breakdown?"

Indeed her chest heaved and she was leaning against a wall. "Betty is insubordinate." She gasped and paused for breath. "I shan't have a maid tell me how to keep discipline in my own home."

Higginson looked questioningly at Betty, who was standing at the entrance to the back door.

"Mr Higginson, I keep a lock on my mouth for a long time but I never throw away the key. Your wife don't have no business treating this child like a stray dog."

"We didn't hire you for your opinions. What don't you like?"

"Your wife throw more abuse on this child than the Soufrière throw ashes when it erupt. And I is tired of the insult—them what Mistress Higginson heaping 'pon this child parents. I sure their ears must be ringing all the time 'cause Mistress is always 'busing them.

Nobody can tell me"—here she lifted both hands above her head and brought them down emphatically—"not even Jesus Christ himself, that half of a penny loaf and a half ounce o' fish and a cup o' tea without milk is enough for a child this size. And when Mistress beat this child for ten minutes 'cause she steal a pancake, when if Mistress uses to give this child enough for eat she wouldn't o' have to steal it, I have to open my mouth and talk. This is wickedness. And if you don't think so, Mr Higginson, you is wicked too, just like your wife." At this point she removed her maid's bonnet and her apron and dropped them onto the kitchen floor. They were the Higginsons' property. "When can I come for my pay?"

"You are not leaving us? Betty?"

"Yes, I is. Your wife done tell me I have to keep my mouth shut even when I see wickedness all around me. Mr Higginson, I don' have money and I don' have eddication, but I have a conscience." Without another word, she was out the door.

Mr Higginson remained speechless for about ten minutes after Betty left. There was a tooting at the gate. The delivery man was impatiently signaling his presence.

Next morning Betty returned. She told Licia that Mr Higginson had sent one of his clerks to ask her to return. And that morning Licia received two penny loaves, an egg, and a cup of hot milk.

After a month the egg was infrequent but the bread and milk continued and occasionally there was a banana or an orange. Sometimes when Mrs Higginson wasn't watching Mr Higginson placed a shilling in Licia's hand. These Licia received with a smile and kept in a jam jar under her cot, until one day Mrs Higginson found them and was about to beat Licia, when Betty corroborated Licia's story.

That August Miss Connie left home to begin her studies in England, and Mrs Higginson began hinting to Betty that there was not enough work for a maid. Someone already did the laundry. Betty took the hint and got a job with another family. For about six months one of Mrs Higginson's poor relatives came twice weekly to help clean the house.

For two years Licia had been preparing breakfast and supper and cleaning the house with only directions from Mrs Higginson. The summer of the second year when Miss Connie came home, she brought Mildred, a twig of a girl, paler than Miss Connie, with blood-red lips, and mustard-coloured hair. The day before, Miss Connie and Mildred had decided to go on a hike two miles away to the seaside grapes. Mrs Higginson told Licia to carry the picnic basket for the girls, to leave it there and to return in the afternoon to fetch it. Licia had carried the basket. But in the meantime Mr Higginson had come home from the store because he wasn't feeling well. When Mrs Higginson said, "Licia, it's time to go fetch the basket," he asked her, "What basket?" She told him. He asked her why Connie could not carry her own picnic basket. Mrs Higginson dropped the doily she was knitting and peered at him over her glasses.

"Look," said Mr. Higginson angrily, "I told you already, Licia is a child. Treat her like a child. I am sick and tired of Licia this, Licia that. She works three times harder than you. We need a maid in this house. This child is neither your slave nor your maid. You and Connie had better get this in your heads." Immediately, Mr Higginson had picked up the phone and told the delivery man to go and pick up the basket.

Half an hour later, when Mr Higginson had gone off to sleep, Mrs Higginson came looking for Licia, "Where are you? There is a lot of tarnished silver here. 'The Devil finds work for idle hands to do.'"

Licia obeyed. She understood that even though Mr. Higginson did not like the way she was treated, he was never there, and so she resolved to try to get along as well as she could with Mrs. Higginson.

～

"Licia, where are you?"

"Here, Mrs. Higginson."

"Can't you find nothing better than to stand on those stones and daydream?"

Licia got down from the stones and walked toward the door.

At fourteen Licia had pointed breasts and full, round hips. Adolescent boys and older men licked their lips when they looked at her. Licia knew this was to be her last year in school. She was not bright enough to win a scholarship or get selected as a trainee teacher, which was more or less the same thing as winning a scholarship. She was bright enough to go to a secondary school but there was no one to pay her school fees.

One evening she heard Mr and Mrs Higginson speaking about her education. Higginson asked how she was doing in school and his wife replied that she wasn't doing badly at all; in fact, she had been surprised that Licia had placed seventh in her class of 40. "Who would have thought Rita and Ansel could produce such a child?" Mr Higginson had suggested sending her to a secondary school. Mrs Higginson said that would be a waste of money; they were getting old; they couldn't throw away their few pennies like this. If Licia proved honest, he could employ her to do little tasks around the store. He did not reply.

Licia's mother was now dead. She had died giving birth to her last baby. Months sometimes went by now before Licia saw her father, and it was usually at a distance.

For several mornings Licia noticed that she was sweating profusely and was constantly nauseous. One morning while Licia was feeling this way Mrs Higginson confronted her.

"Licia did you use any napkins this month? I don't recall your asking me for any."

"I didn't need any."

"What are you saying, child? Have you been doing anything with boys?"

Licia bowed her head.

"'From the throes of the evil one, Good Lord, deliver us!' Go pack your things! You are leaving the house this very minute."

"Why do you have to be always screaming at this child?"

"Malcolm, I think Licia is in the family way."

"No, no! Didn't you warn her about that?"

"I saw no need to."

Mr Higginson shook his head and sucked his teeth in dismay. "Anyway, you aren't sure. Let Dr Anderson examine her."

So Licia went to see Dr Anderson, who confirmed that she was pregnant. He phoned the information to Mrs Higginson while Licia was still in his office.

Mrs Higginson was waiting at the gate when Licia arrived. She had all Licia's belongings stuffed in a pillow case. "Don't come back here. You will cause a curse to descend on this house." She locked the gate and returned inside.

Licia simply sat at the gate and cried. People passed and saw her, and the sun got higher and higher. She felt someone tapping her. It was Mother Bell—a strapping, jet-black woman in her seventies, in a loose dress of red and white plaids and a headtie of the same material. Two thick white braids hung down the side of her face. With one hand Mother Bell steadied herself against the wall, with the other she held the cane with which she was tapping Licia.

"Get up, child. What's wrong?" Licia did not get up and she did not answer right away."

"Mrs Higginson put me . . ."

"—out," Mother Bell completed the sentence. "Ain't you Rita daughter?"

Licia nodded without lifting her gaze from the ground.

"So why Miss Higginson run you?"

Licia did not answer.

"Was you rude to her?"

Licia shook her head.

"Don't tell me! O Lord, don't tell me! I think I suspect." The grandmother eased herself down beside Licia. She pulled a rag from her pocket and wiped Licia eyes. "Who is the father?"

Licia did not answer.

"Ain't you going to have a baby?"

Licia said nothing.

Suddenly Licia's eyes bulged, and she began to howl. "I will kill myself!"

Mother Bell pulled her towards her and buried her head in her dress. "Dry your tears, child. This is time for thinking, not crying."

Reality came to Licia. Pallo had touched her breasts sometimes and it made a current go through her body and he had kissed her on the lips and made her feel dizzy and every recess she and Pallo used to go the cemetery and lie down behind a clump of bushes and Pallo used to unbutton his trousers and tell her to play with his "thing" and white juice used to come out of it and Pallo used to hold on tight to her when it was coming out and one day Pallo told her to take off her bloomers and he pushed his thing into her and she hollered and he put his hand over her mouth and there was blood and she was frightened and she didn't let Pallo do that to her again for another month and that time was all right and one day when he was doing it she felt her whole body grow stiff and a current moving through her and what a sensation and she loved it and so much so that she planned how to let Pallo into her room at night and he used to climb over the wall and she used to tie a string to her big toe and leave it hanging out the window and he would pull the string and she would let him in through the window. She should have known. At school they told one another, "What sweet nanny goat does swell she gut."

Mother Bell led her to the Higginson store while Licia thought about all this. Higginson knew Mother Bell very well. She was a highly respected, retired midwife. Higginson nodded and then shook his head when he saw the pillow case and Licia's tear-stained face. He motioned Mother Bell to come to the back of the store. When Mother Bell returned, she took Licia home with her.

Mother Bell lived in a wooden house that was better than most. It had two bedrooms, a living room and an enclosed porch where she did her own cooking on a two-burner kerosene stove. In the mornings and afternoons one of the neighbours' children brought her a bucket of water from the nearby standpipe. Another of the neighbours did her laundry. Once or twice a day she emptied her chamber pot in the outhouse at the back. Mother Bell only went out when she had to see the doctor or cash the money orders her two daughters, nurses in America, sent her. Licia's coming to live with her was a blessing, and she told Licia so.

Mr Higginson had arranged with Mother Bell to pay for Licia's living expenses. Each week Licia went to the store for a supply of groceries and each month he gave her a small sum of money, which he increased when the baby was born.

When Pallo found out that Licia was pregnant he shunned her. He himself was only sixteen. In fact, he should not have been in primary school. He told Licia that his mother had sent him to school two years late, and she had reduced his age accordingly. Before the child was born, he hinted to Licia that he did not want to be named its father; if acknowledging the child meant that he had to give her money, he would say it was not his. Licia's shock had opened her eyes sufficiently for her to realize that Pallo's attitude was commonplace. Eventually Pallo stopped visiting her. When the baby was born he did not come to see it.

When her daughter was almost three years, Pallo came to see her one evening to tell her that an uncle of his in England had made arrangements for him to immigrate to England. He told her that it was really because he had no money to give the child that he had stopped coming to see her. He promised that she would see a change once he went to England and found a job. Licia did not believe him.

Mother Bell's health had declined during the first three years Licia lived with her, and not long after Pallo left for England, she died. Licia continued to live in her house.

Pallo had not been in England for a full year, when he asked Licia to join him, provided she did not bring the child. She discussed Pallo's request with Mr Higginson. He told her that he found it quite hard to advise her. He did not like the idea of Licia abandoning her child to someone else's care, but he appreciated the fact that Pallo wished to marry her, "make an honourable woman of you." He offered to pay the baby's fare to England if that were the problem. But Pallo's explanation was that he was a student and he also wanted Licia to resume her studies and he felt that the baby would be in the way. Mr Higginson blinked his eyes several times when Licia told him this. Finally he smiled and said, "That's wonderful!" Eventually he arranged with one of the ex-maids to look after Marge, and Licia was able to leave for England.

Licia had hardly been a month in England, when the woman who was caring for Marge had a stroke. Mr Higginson took Marge home to Mrs Higginson. He laid down the rules. No abuse. Marge must have her own bedroom. She was not to be groomed as anybody's maid. The maid who had come to replace Licia was to stay and if she left she was to be replaced.

Mrs Higginson surprised him. She took up the little child, now four, and cuddled her. She began making frilly dresses for her, and took her to church on Sundays; she began teaching her to read, and she proposed sending her to the same private school Miss Connie had attended.

Licia could not believe what she was reading in Mr Higginson's letters. She could not understand the change that had come over Mrs. Higginson.

II

The house was hushed. Everyone walked around on tiptoe. They hesitated before opening drawers or closets. Connie, Mrs Higginson, and Marge spoke more in gestures than in words; and when words came they made only half sentences—a nod, a shake of the head, or floral opening of the palms said the rest. Doctor Anderson came in the morning and again at six in the evening.

Three days before, Dr Anderson had suggested a live-in nurse, and he himself had hired the retired but very spry Gertie Sauls. Gertie performed her tasks with well-timed movements and followed every procedure with the punctuality of a clock. She reigned over the sick room like a tyrant, even denying the family access to it. Just before Dr Anderson arrived, she had told a tearful Connie, "You can't go in there! The last thing he wants is someone to depress his spirits. Let your father rest."

Every time Dr Anderson came out of the room, Mrs Higginson would meet him at the door and stare directly into his pupils for news. Dr Anderson would direct his gaze to the floor. Connie and Marge observed this scene from a distance. Now, however, Dr Anderson spoke. "He wants to have a talk with all three of you. Go in, he's waiting."

The three women entered the room, which was heavy with the

scent of the red roses Father Kirby had sent that morning. Mr Higginson was in a half-sitting position, supported on all sides with pillows. The drapes in the bedroom were drawn, but that didn't hide his ashen colour. His sky-blue pyjamas didn't help either.

Mrs Higginson stood to the right of the bed. She took his hand in hers, and tears welled up in her eyes. Connie stood on the left side and looked on quietly. Marge stood at the foot of the bed. Mr Higginson looked at Marge, now fourteen. He smiled and Marge smiled too.

"I haven't had time to notice how big and beautiful you've grown."

Marge's smile grew wider, and both Connie and Mrs Higginson looked at Marge and smiled too.

"I am thirsty. Marge, would you like to bring Papa some water."

"Certainly," and she went out of the room. She returned with a silver tray on which was the covered glass of water and a napkin.

"Now, Connie, you give me a hand here." He indicated his left. "And, Amelia, you give me one on your side."

They both lifted him into a sitting position, and Marge held the glass to his lips. When he had finished, she dabbed his lips with the napkin.

"Now let me lie down again." They eased him gently back.

He turned his eyes to the wall and spoke as if to himself, "Licia should be here." This was followed by a long silence during which he kept his eyes closed.

He opened his eyes and said, "I have a lot to say and I want everyone of you to hear it all. Come closer, Marge." He held her hand. "Give me yours too, Constance. You are both my daughters: Connie, you my flesh and blood; Marge, you by adoption; and I love you both equally." He paused. "Now move a little to the foot of the bed. I want to see your faces while I say what I must. I know some people think highly of me. Now that I am about to die, I want that opinion destroyed." He paused lengthily and looked as though examining the scarlet petals of the roses and smiled. "All my life I have been a hypocrite and a thief."

Mrs Higginson gasped and looked at Marge.

"No, Amelia," he said detachedly, "she stays. You must all hear it . . . My father left Scotland because he had embezzled the firm for which he worked as an accountant. He stowed away on a ship sailing to the West Indies, and, thanks to a black man who discovered him but did not turn him in and brought him food and scouted the decks for him, he made it to Dominica alive.

"He arrived there about forty years after the abolition of slavery, and by then a few Blacks had managed to acquire some money and were buying crown lands. My father had some legal training and so he set up a law practice. It was he who drew up the deeds for those people, except that the deeds were all drawn up in my father's name, and what he gave to those people were contracts saying that they were going to work the land for him. The people had all put their "X"s on those documents. Several years later, when it was convenient for him, my father sold those lands to an overseas coffee company and took the money and came to Isabella Island.

"Here he bought land and started the store I own today. Later he came to Scotland to get me. I was an adolescent of eighteen then and was living with my grandmother. He brought me here and I worked in the store while he shared his time between the store and the land he had acquired. He gave half of that land to the Anglican Church. They've long sold it. I sold my half, 120 acres, and put the money into stocks." There were beads of sweat on his forehead, and his voice had grown slightly faint. Marge went to the head of the bed and wiped his brow.

"And yet my father was such a highly respected man—a justice of the peace, a warden in the church. He used to say to me, 'Malcolm, watch out, you have a tendency to be overkind. In the jungle of life your claws have got to be bloody to survive, and the predator cannot feel sorry for the prey.' He became ill, bedridden for several months, and at night I used to hear him scream, 'Stop him! He's coming to get me!' And the housekeeper and I would ask him who, and he would look at us and repeat 'Who?' Sometimes he said a big, black man kept laughing and cracking a whip menacingly at him. I think he gave that land to the church as a way of finding peace within his soul, but he didn't find it. The night before he died, he told me of all the evil things he had done. Towards morning we heard him screaming, 'I'm not going! The flames! Help! Help!' By the time we got to his bedside, he had already stopped breathing.

"My father's deeds have weighed heavily on me since I found out about them. I married a black woman, for I felt that whatever I inherited should revert to the black race—that I had to make peace with Blacks, atone for my father's wrongs. But if I had been courageous I would have given it all away after my father's death." He took a long pause and stared at the ceiling.

"I won't be in this world long and I won't be leaving anything for the church as my father's conscience made him do. I stole it from the people. I must give it back to the people."

"What! Papa!" Connie exclaimed.

He lifted his hand in a plea for silence. "I called you to listen to me. Dr Anderson is the executor of my will. I have left enough, Amelia, to make sure you don't suffer in your last days. There's a little something for you, Connie. Marge, I have left enough to provide for six years of university education for you and a little extra for afterwards.

"The bulk of my wealth is bequeathed to the community to build some social facility. I have left them the choice.

"I want no final communion rites. I'm not a believer."

Mrs Higginson gasped.

"No, I have never been. Where is God when the helpless are raped, robbed, persecuted? Where is he, Ameilia? But going to church has never been a problem. I loved the hymns, I loved hearing the nonsense those rascals preached. We sat comfortably in our pews. Amelia, dear, everything white isn't pious.

"Connie, come hold my hand."

Connie moved to the head of the bed and he seized her right hand. "I hope you find a wonderful husband. The colour of his skin must not matter. Put aside your mother's nonsense or you will find life very burdensome.

"Come, Marge, come kiss me goodbye." He held her wrist with his left hand.

She kissed him and patted his forehead with her free hand.

There was a long, ominous silence in which one became aware of the massive mahogany furniture in the room, stained almost black, and the grim portraits of dead people on the bedroom walls, broken finally by Mrs Higginson's sobs.

"What are you crying for, Amelia?"

"Your soul, Malcolm, your soul."

"No need to worry, Amelia. I've settled that a long time ago. I've never wronged God. He doesn't exist. I've wronged people. I don't believe in heaven or hell."

"O, Malcolm, I wish you wouldn't say that! Your blasphemy cuts me to the bone."

He didn't answer but turned his eyes to the ceiling. One could see that there was a detail he was trying to remember. "One last thing: the instructions for my burial are locked with my will in the vault. Dr Anderson knows the combination. Connie, Amelia, Marge kiss me goodbye."

They did.

Suddenly he became quite irritable. "Call the nurse, and please leave. I am very tired."

They all sat in the living room, too stunned to talk. Mrs Higginson looked fixedly at an imaginary spot outside the window where there was only darkness. Somewhere in the town a group of barking dogs were chasing something, and the night breeze whistled through the leaves of the royal palms outside the windows.

The six-foot grandfather clock in the corner at the living room entrance from the foyer gave eleven sonorous gongs. Connie rose and led her mother to the guest room where she now slept . A while later Marge rose and went to her room.

That night Mr Higginson died. Two days later he was buried in the Anglican churchyard.

III

Marge asked the taxi driver to take her directly to the church where the funeral procession was entering. She walked up to the front pew, where only the family was allowed to sit. Momentarily she did not recognize Connie, now Mrs Gresham, divorced, and mother of a seven-year-old son and a five-year-old daughter. Hanging jowls, puffy bags under her eyes, an unusually red face. Marge had heard Connie was heavy into the bottle.

It had to have been a sudden death. Just like Grandma to stipulate that she wanted a next-day burial and inconvenience others. Someone had come all the way to Trinity College to give her the message. All British Airways flights to the Caribbean had already left. No, she could not get to the Caribbean before the following afternoon. But they could take her number and see whether a continental carrier had anything. Would she be ready at a minute's notice? Yes, there was a possibility. Could she be at Gatwick in three hours? Yes, she would take a cab! Okay, she could catch a late flight to Martinique. She could get a 7 AM flight from Martinique to Isabella Island. By 8 AM she should be home. But the flight from Martinique was an hour late, so she knew she had to go directly to the church.

Connie did not acknowledge her bow. Marge sang the funeral hymns and listened to the praise showered on Grandma. She remembered Grandma's soothing fingers on her feverish face, she remembered the nights she'd had trouble falling asleep and how Grandma's singing would calm her, and she also remembered the quarrel between Grandma and Connie over the "bastard brat on whom you lavish so much attention. You didn't on her mother." The tears trickled down her face, for she felt the beginnings of the space Grandma's death would create.

Mrs Higginson was buried in the churchyard beside her husband.

Marge's second attempt to speak to Connie was rebuffed. Connie took her two children and left the churchyard as soon as the burial ceremony was over.

Several people, including Dr Anderson's wife, came to speak to Marge. Isabel, Mrs Higginson's niece, stood a little apart from them and gestured that she was waiting to speak to Marge.

After the well-wishers and sympathizers had moved away, Marge went over to where Isabel stood. After greeting Isabel, she asked why Connie was behaving so strangely. "You mustn't mind her. It has to do with her mother's will. I know all about it. My husband was Aunt Amelia's attorney. Where are you staying?"

"You know, I had assumed it would be at the Higginson house. It is as if I had expected to go there and still find Grandma there."

"Well, it's clear that you won't be welcome. Besides, Connie moved back there when her marriage broke up. Why don't you stay with me?"

"Why not? Thank you so much."

"Let's go to the rectory and collect your things."

By 5 PM Marge had rested up, and she and Isabel were having tea on the front balcony of Isabel's house.

"A strange woman Aunt Amelia was. Imagine dividing up her property equally among you, Licia, and Connie. Connie won't be getting that house." She took a swallow of tea. "You know"— she was staring intensely into the teacup—"there was a bizarre change in Aunt Amelia's behaviour in her last years. You might be able to help me throw some light on that. Just before her husband died, she started being nice to us. Daddy couldn't understand it, because for close to thirty years she'd deliberately avoided us. She didn't like Mother. Aunt Amelia had trouble liking or respecting anyone with a black skin, and you know Mother is black. But we couldn't understand the sudden change. Do you know why she changed so suddenly?"

"People change," Marge said nonchalantly. "We're told to respect our elders because they are wise. Grandma probably got wise in her old age. Maybe it was the fear of death; she was making sure she wouldn't be excluded from heaven." Marge remembered the concern she had expressed for her husband's soul.

"I'm not convinced, Marge. Isn't there something you are hiding from me? There's got to be more than that."

"No, nothing, nothing that I know of. I could ask the same question myself. You know how Grandma treated my mother. You know how she treated me. What accounted for the difference? Maybe some people see truth while they are young and others must wait until they're old."

"I don't believe that, Marge. Some people have to be shocked before they change. Aunt Amelia was one of those people. I would like to know what caused her to change. Marge, I feel that you know why."

Marge shook her head, and thought of a conversation she'd had with her mother and father at the supper table two years earlier. She had gone down from Oxford to London to have supper with her parents and later go to see a play. Her mother had talked about the difficulties of being a social worker in Brixton and was envying her husband for what she called his cushy civil service position before changing the subject. "Marge, there's something I must tell you. It's good to know these things. They can prevent problems down the road. Mrs Higginson's brother Edgar came to see me when he was in England twelve years ago for Isabel's graduation. He told me, 'Licia, I'm your father. I've noticed the resemblance between you and my mother, and I've not known how to own up to what I did. Your mother used to be our helper and I used to have sex with her. True, she was living with your father, but . . . '"

Marge looked at Isabel. Evidently her father had never told his children that Licia was their sister. Perhaps he had told Amelia. Perhaps that had accounted for the change in her. There was no way of knowing how much was known. Wouldn't it be interesting for her to tell Isabel, *Do you know that I am your niece?* But that could raise more problems than it would solve. Let Licia do that herself.

"Isabel, I agree with you that there's a lot concerning your Aunt Amelia that we don't know. Maybe Connie has some of the answers. But look at it this way, Grandma is already dead, and our knowledge won't alter anything."

Caleb's Tempest

CALEB VAUX, WHO SOMETIMES KNOWS he's Caliban Veau, sits on one side of a table that is in a tiny alcove off a large room. Damp dust, mingled with the fumes of yellowing paper piled in stacks, is everywhere. At the far end of the room, where the printer and his assistant are moving around, the unvarnished floor boards creak incessantly. It's November 17, 3:30 PM, but on account of the pouring rain, it's almost dark outside. The windows are closed, and sweat pours down from everyone; even from Horatio Pemberton, son of the proprietor of *The Isabellan* and heir to a five-thousand-acre plantation and one of Isabella Island's two national banks.

Five years ago Caleb's father Percival had been forced to sell *The Isabellan*—a weekly ragtag Caleb secretly called it and no grail holy or profane but a sieve—because he had borrowed heavily to send Caleb's older brother Carl to London University to study economics and elevate the family's status. Carl upon graduation would have repaid the loan. But he died of leukemia *or the burden of his name in St Mary's Hospital so the doctors said but it was poison said*

Pixie their servant whom Caleb calls circus Picadilly. Shango Shaker Picadilly had a vision a snake's head in Carl's mouth body wrapped around his body she didn't want to tell anything but the absolute truth so help her god who told her to tell this vision only to Caleb.

Piccadilly laughs at Percival, who for years has come home each day at four, donned white clothes and a bowler, sat on the verandah he built outside the house that he inherited from his pa—close to the neighbours, but thank God they d no longer empty their chamberpots from their windows—and shouts so they—who don't have servants but are servants to faraway rich people—hear him order his tea and just as loud afterwards say, "Pixie, you make the most excellent tea, and that pastry, dear, is heavenly-just-heavenly," whether or not there has been pastry. And if he's in the mood, he pulls Pixie into his bedroom.

So surrounded is the house by shacks that although they're on the top of the hill that overlooks the harbour half a mile below, they cannot see the sea—and the neighbours' quarrels and the smells of their cooking are poor substitutes.

Some years the British give Pa Vaux a piece of brass with dangling ribbons and benight him commander of something or the other and put him in order or disorder or something or the other that he goes to receive when he should be spraying the termites slowly eating away at the foundation of the house. *A fond old man in his kingdom barred from the sea and without daughters to turn him out of doors so he might learn wisdom.*

Horatio Pemberton sits on the other side of the table. It's Thursday. He comes every Thursday whenever he's in the colony to check the contents of that week's edition, to change a word or a paragraph before the Grammarian comes early Friday morning to see that English is kept up. *Got to keep English up, it might fall down like undies in a public place.*

The Isabellan, all sixteen twelve-by-eighteen pages, is spread out on the table. Horatio Pemberton is interested in one page only. Grammatical mistakes are permissible in the others. He marks away with his yellow felt pen, just a shade brighter than his hair. He lifts his head and opens fully the two tiny blue electric light bulbs in his lobster-red face tanned by the days spent on his father's golf and tennis courts. Horatio is twenty-two.

"There are things here the Grammarian won't approve of." He points the highlighter to some of the words he has underlined. "This paragraph, and this other one, they have a sort of a—I can't find the word—ring to them. Ah yes. Subversive. They should be excised. What's their purpose, anyway? All that trash happened before you and I were born. It doesn't concern us. Take it out. That would be all." His six-feet of mostly white muslin rises and quickly leaves. *Before you and I were born*—clipped British accent—the cock in wait to take over the coop.

Caleb Vaux is forty-two and hasn't yet received the mantle from Papa Vaux *who is Methodist turned Anglican* for profit. Caleb had just been hired by his father when Horatio Pemberton was born. He had covered the birth because there was a tradition that came from somewhere powerful that said you covered everything significant in the lives of the five families with plantations of over three thousand acres. Well, not all the events: if the bride had been pregnant at the time of marriage you took the photograph to betray the fact, and you did not write about their brown and black mistresses, some of whom unknown to them were their own kin. Pa Vaux had rewritten the article about Horatio's birth, adding to it the detail that said Horatio was the fourth generation to carry the name.

Though of humble station, I feel confident that the magnanimous Sir Isaac Pemberton will not take aught amiss over my speculation that the name was inspired by the illustrious Horatio Nelson. And what an apt name it is for the most outstanding and exemplary of families! Pre-eminent contributors to the commonweal of Isabellans. . . .

Papa Vaux, now there's a cock that knows when to crow. Papa Vaux had written something too about their horse-racing skills, the perfection of which they were never loathe to leave off to open clinics, police stations, or to inspect the militia, but the Grammarian had considered it an excrescence and left it blood-red.

Horatio Nelson Pemberton the fourth, future cutter of ribbons at newly established military training posts, lived most of the time in England. Several times each year *The Isabellan* proclaimed his arrivals and departures as well as those of other Pembertons, the Haliburtons, the Dufferins, the Moodys, the Sewalls and the Colchesters (some of whom had under two thousand acres).

Departing from the colony yesterday accompanied by his governess was young Master Horatio Pemberton. The young Pemberton begins his first year of elementary school at St John's Academy in Kent, one of England's five most distinguished schools and alma mater of many of Britain's statesmen, aristocrats, and royals.

Asked how he thinks he would like his stay away from home, the genial heir beamed his blue eyes, shook his golden curls, looked furtively at his governess, and said, "I shall like it very much."

The Isabellan *wishes Master Horatio Pemberton abundant success.*

* * *

Arriving home from England for the Easter break, departing for England for the fall term accompanied by his mother, Isabella Island's wealthiest heir . . .

* * *

Farting, thinking that he could not be heard, was the young getting-to-be-an-adolescent Horatio the fourth Pemberton. And the servants heard and smelled it and were quite surprised that Horatio the fourth Pemberton actually farted and that it stank.

That had not been published but he hadn't destroyed it and Pa Vaux had found it and clouted him, "You fucking jackass!" (The printers had already gone for the day.) "What you trying to do? Shut the fucking paper down!" His left hand fingering the ribbons of two of those brass things the Queen gives him on her birthday that they say are for long and faithful service. The right hand reaching into his coat pocket—a grey tweed affair stinking of sweat but which he always wore—pulling out his soda pills and tossing down a few, his face wearing that screwed-up look that always followed this activity, its lines deepening, its molasses-colour darkening. Caleb was grateful that the old man had stopped asking if they wanted him to lose the other half of his gut. "You blasted ingrates and bloodsuckers" was also less frequent, for at that time Carl was in his second year at LSE.

The Anglican Cathedral bell has already chimed seven times. Caleb can no longer put off tackling the paragraphs that are to be removed. He'd already struck out a lot from the piece in anticipation of the objections of Horatio the fourth Pemberton and the Grammarian, who once ran red lines through a paragraph of an article Caleb had written on the primary school teachers' strike. The paragraph had read:

The president of the Teachers Fraternity, Mr. Alfred Jacobs, claimed that the Colonial Bureau of Education refused to talk to him. Each time he telephoned, the receiver was slammed in his ear, and when he went in person to meet the senior civil servant of the bureau, two thugs met him at the door, took him down to the police station and roughed him up.

The Grammarian had said, "This passage is disproportioned in matter and in style. I shall emend it handsomely."

The secretary for Her Majesty's Schools on Isabella Island, the distinguished Sir Peter Crow, OBE, KCMG, informed The Isabellan yesterday that Alfred Jacobs, the head of the teacher mob, came to Her Majesty's Government Buildings and demanded to see him. When Sir Peter went out to meet him, Jacobs began to point his finger in Sir Peter's face and to hurl violent imprecations at the person of that distinguished gentleman. The police were forced to intervene to protect Sir Peter's person. Several witnesses have corroborated Sir Peter's story.

This had been the first year of the Pemberton proprietorship. It wouldn't have mattered anyway: Pa Vaux would have allowed it and quickly toss down a few soda tablets afterwards. *I should have burned their books and gabble like a thing most brutish.*

Well, Isabella Island is going to be independent in another week, but it had already been in charge of its internal affairs when Major Archibald Prospero, the Grammarian, a colossal, pink-skinned gentleman with blue blotches on his leering face, and who carries part of himself in a black attaché case—had altered the article, and Caleb had known better than to appeal to the Chief Minister—infected with Columbitis. *A happy nigger is he to wanton Whites, who use him in their sports: "Oi is they equal, man, Oi dress in whoite and play cricket better than any whoite man."*

"Gosh, man, I thought that time you got hit, they said they mistook you for the wicket."

The British, who'd engineered his election, had got him to rubber-stamp a boiler-plate constitution that most people would never read. But Pa Vaux had read it and bled from his ulcer the entire night. "Every white fool and his grandson and great-grandson who ever touched these shores will get pensions from the taxes of people who need those taxes to give themselves clean drinking water, people who have to walk five miles and stand in line for half a day to see a doctor. And that Calabash-head of a Quashee grinned like a fucking Sambo, signed it, and never even read it."

Pa Vaux, in this one instance you frowned at the termites and black blood bled from your bottom.

This paragraph. To change or not to change, that is the question. No, not a question but an imperial order from St Michael and St George designed to get your saintly gorge if you had any left.

Grammar! Looking for the majestic in her majesty's schools dan is the man in the van let me hold your hand see dick run what see what runs from dick jane saw a stain on the window pane spell pane p a i n not that pane you lame-brain.

Can't take a chance. A Grammarian to keep English up. Some fear things may fall and never rise. Take hold of yourself, Caleb. It ain't— oops: isn't—so bad being a journalist and editor of *The Isabellan*. You get to know the truth even if you can't print or repeat it. And at election time—they should have elections more often—you could earn more than a year's salary. Joseph Harry, opposition leader not yet a thief and bleeder but certainly a liar and definitely hated by Pemberton and their scarecrow Petered-out Whiteham, brought his panting three hundred pounds up the stairs to the office just before the last election, and I, afraid he'd have a heart attack, pray until he gets his breath. It's about the article on my desk—picture and all of the thirteen-year-old mistress Joseph has. They all have. Principals marrying or putting out of their schools thirteen-year olds pregnant for them. Wonder how much Pemberton and Whiteham paid her for the picture and story? Certainly more than Joe Ha-ha (Whiteham calls him that) gives her for the usual favours. "Harry make me have a abortion. . ." her signed statement began.

"How much will you pay?"

"Five hundred dollars."

I shake my head. *That won't do. I ain't no coonoomoonoo. You'll pay me sucker, if you don't want me to say boo.* "Five grand, in good old Abe Lincoln, nothing else and not a penny less."

Looks like lice biting you, man, I want to say. Never saw a body fidget so.

"G'ie me a break, man. Think o' the blessings that will drop your way when I take power."

I laugh. *Not a chance, Joe Ha-ha.*

He pushes his hand in his jacket pocket and pulls out a cheque book. I shake my head. "Legal tender. Abe Lincoln, nothing else and not a penny less."

He leaves, promising to come back in twenty minutes, and he does, and I am US$5,000 richer. They should have elections more often. Better for democracy too.

Pemby gave me shit for not printing it. And for a little while he'd have wrung my neck and had me cooked if he'd had another rooster for the coop. But what did they teach me language for, if not to lie?— like if most of what language says is truth. Fifty dollars to each printer to say the equipment broke down and the photograph couldn't be printed. What's a story without a photo? You tell me. A journalist has

got to be thorough. *Une image vaut mille mots.* The election took
place the following Tuesday. No point printing it after the election.
Whiteham won anyway. The omitted article at least gave Isabella
Island an opposition and Joe Ha-ha won his seat. The fourth estate.
Some pay you to print, others to not print, still others pay you to
print what others have already paid you not to print. Got to be careful
though with Pemby's protégés. That one with the opposition leader
was a close shot and it was me and not his words Pemby minced when
he told me so.

They ain't paying me enough. It ain't a thousand acres I want.
WATCH YOUR GRAMMAR! Only to keep a car, pay for a good time
with a woman, and go on a drunk from time to time. Salary can't even
give me that. Luckily I'm not a father, which is not to say there aren't
women saying that I'm the father of their children. A man's got to
have some fun. The sun runs—re-runs. And time duns. Good rhymes
those. Good for Miss Beckles with Her Majesty's readers that create
thoughtless excellent spellers. Miss Beckles with her uncrossed legs . .
. *a stain in the window pane spell pane p a i n you lame-brain.*

The article stares at him. Begin at the beginning. Not in *Medias res.*
The fun's always in the middle. Begin at the beginning:

*The lead-up to nationhood goes on apace. Every day now history
is made. Fifteen persons who had been imprisoned "for gross crimes
against Her Majesty's government"* (the asshole Horatio Pemberton,
fourth of the jackasses, had run his highlighter through the quotation
marks) *were released yesterday as a testimony of Her Majesty's goodwill
toward the emerging nation. Sir Abraham Bhatt, Her Majesty's gover-
nor and representative, was there to address the prisoners, who came out
one by one and were told: "Her Majesty pardons you . . . ."*

*His honour graciously shook the hands of each of the released. Their
names . . .* (He skips that part and moves on to the next paragraph)

These people were convicted and imprisoned thirty-two years ago over an issue which at the time was fraught with controversy. They had set fire to and burned down several of the colonists' homes and businesses. An Englishwoman was asphyxiated. The fire was in response to the alleged rape of Beulah Costello, whose father had killed the alleged rapist, a lieutenant in her Majesty's militia. Her Majesty's court had found that no rape had been committed and had hanged the girl's father for murdering the lieutenant. Angered by this decision, the residents of Lower Town had marched to the Colonial Administration Building and begun setting it on fire. Five of their number were killed by the militia and another twenty arrested and sentenced to life imprisonment for the death of the asphyxiated woman.

Several of the outstanding citizens of our soon-to-be nation were present at the pardoning. Our Chief Minister, Sir Peter Whiteham, expressed his gratitude for the gesture of goodwill extended by her Majesty and appreciation for the contented look on the faces of the released. He closed his speech with the Biblical citation: "'Render unto Caesar the things that are Caesar's and to God the things that are God's" but added, "Today Caesar has shown leniency but it must not be taken as a sign of things to come—when this Caesar holds the reins and applies the spurs."

There are yellow lines drawn through those paragraphs. *What the fuck am I to write?* And that isn't one quarter of the story. He was ten when the rape occurred. But yesterday Papa Vaux, who had attended the ceremony, told him the entire story. Pa Vaux had attended the trial, had spoken with the prosecuting and defense attorneys, and knew all the off-the-record views but could publish only the typewritten bulletins issued by the police commissioner. Anything else, they had told him, and he'd be charged with seditious libel and the paper would be banned. During the trial Dr Smith had visited Pa Vaux. Smith was a mulatto, an out-of-marriage son of one of the

Colchesters, whose name he couldn't carry. He was the only doctor available to the nonwhite population of Hanovertown. Smith had visited Pa Vaux two nights after the murder. He wanted to know whether Pa Vaux's paper could help him. Smith had wanted to take a stand. The Police Commissioner, he said, had held a gun to his head and told him to tear up the report he had written after examining Beulah, who was sixteen. There had been blood on her undergarments and the lieutenant's sperms were in her. That's what he had written. With the gun to his head, he was made to sign a document that read,

After a thorough examination of the relevant parts of Miss Beulah Costello's anatomy, I find no evidence to suggest that the young lady had been sexually molested. While it is evident that she has already had sexual intercourse, nothing indicates that she has engaged in any such activity within the last few days.

"I couldn't help Smith," Pa Vaux told Caleb. "We'd known each other since secondary school days. His father had arranged for him to study medicine. I, as you've heard me say time and again, shouldn't have gone to secondary school. Joe Hicks and I were the only true Negroes in that school. Everybody else was white or off-white. Smith was a good fellow. Always was. But I couldn't help him. Long before the verdict came down he left Isabella Island. I always felt he ran for his life. In those days whenever you knew anything they were uncomfortable with and they couldn't count on you to keep your mouth shut, they took you out."

The day Alban Costello was found guilty of murder and sentenced to be hanged, fire was set to the storage depot at the wharf and to every major store in the capital. Altogether sixty buildings were destroyed. A wonder, only one person died. The five people who were shot and the twenty (five of the prisoners had died in the interim) who were sentenced to life imprisonment had been attempting to set fire to the Colonial Administration Building. They couldn't get to the British Administrator's residence. An unscalable fence surrounded it, and a dozen armed militia had been posted at strategic points around it.

Pa Vaux said he was ashamed of some of the releases he'd had to publish. One was about the animal instincts *"which are preponderant in the uncivilized. These [having] gained the upper hand in the colony, nothing but a firm hand can control it. Anyone caught engaging in subversive activity will be shot on sight. We regret this, but see it as a temporary setback in our task to uplift the benighted."*

After the trial they had gone on to arrest all persons who prior to the outbreak of the trouble had voiced any dissent against colonial rule. Percy Brown, a mulatto who owned a pharmacy and was urging the plantation workers to unionize, was arrested and his pharmacy set on fire. From their hiding places Brown's sons watched the Police Commissioner pour the gasoline and strike the match. On the plantations the workers who so much as grumbled about their wages were fired. And Papa Vaux could publish none of this.

Poor Papa Vaux.

Caleb Vaux, waiting to receive the mantle from Papa Vaux, returns to the article in front of him. What choice does he have? *Tread softly. . . . Let it alone, you fool.*

Excise the damn thing. We are such stuff as dreams are made of. *It's going on nine o'clock. I'm getting sleepy and a chick is waiting for me. No Miranda. No virgin knot of which I need be solicitous. Not quite as I like it but for tonight she'll do. Can't change the world. Got to live in it and have fun.* I will be wise hereafter and seek for grace. *After independence. This island's not mine. . .* My forebears came here chained for labour and to carry out the chainers' orders. Ah, Monsieur Prospero, you taught me language—or think you did—and I dare not curse you—not publicly. Besides, I'm a son of Percival Vaux, aka Archie Bootlicker. No matter.

The Headmaster's Visit

THESE GODDAMN WAVES NEVER STOP! They pound and pound this cursed shore like cannons forever discharging. Standing in the middle of his living room and rubbing his hands, the headmaster was nervous. The oversized grey trousers he wore were held up by red suspenders. His ballooned stomach gave a globelike roundness to his pelvis. A white, long-sleeved shirt, a grey silk tie, and brown kid leather shoes completed his attire. His brown, round face was circled by lines that left two prominent clefts under his chin. He still had a few patches of grey stubble at the back and sides of his head. A fraying black string hung beside his right cheek, the loose end detached from his bifocals.

12:30, he thought. That young man will soon be here. Since he had invited him to visit, memories had begun to replay themselves, as if the invitation were a psychic emetic, and he did not like what he was vomiting. *The ghostly moonlight on the brown unharvested arrowroot fields sloping down to the glowing streak of a river below . . . the wind rustling the almond leaves . . . the occasional hoots of an owl . . . woman was made for man . . . ready soon as they have breasts . . . foolish to prevent ewes in heat from doing it . . . damn society for making me feel guilty . . . she wasn't any good . . . had to tickle her to make her move . . . unqualified for her teaching job . . . a poor screw . . . should have been let go at the end of the year except if I could use her services . . . that education officer was good with words . . . gave damn poor service under the almond tree those nights in the bright moonlight . . . did it like a fucking corpse . . . kept her on staff for two full years long-suffering fool that I am . . . tell that to my wife . . . did nothing exciting for my staff.*

"Woman will send you to the madhouse," Percy said . . . *canefield was on fire . . . ran and left Simone there . . . flames behind me flames in front of me . . . got to the road hands bleeding from blade cuts . . . didn't see Simone for days . . . canestalk ripped her dress . . . wasn't burned.*

Saw Beulah, Bibo's woman, this morning. Wondered if she's still a sweet grind. Shaped like an S. Breasts like two pieces of twine. Could tie a man with them though. Whoever knows the book by its cover? Got to taste, got to taste to know what's bitter, what's sweet, what's brackish. Lord, SHE was SWEET! *Threw those legs around your back . . . wattle-and-daub shack too small to stretch my legs in . . . that was what you called action . . . kept going like a hand pump down there . . . just clutched and clutched and made you bawl out . . . you hit heaven and just like a suction pump pulling every drop of juice out of you . . . you lay there stunted afterwards . . . when you got up you staggered.*

Except for the night Bibo entered cowcod in his hand . . . and down there clutching I had to choose between coming and running . . . stretched out my legs pushed out a wall . . . outside naked running . . . they nicknamed me Pendulum from the way my balls swung.

He went to stand at the window and looked past the swaying palms at the dark blue, angry waters of the Atlantic, at the hillocks where the waves crested, at the numerous whitecaps and flecks of linear foam, the billows pounding the black sand like charging bulls. There was such a sameness to this sea, a sameness, a stability he craved all his life. Of late, that section farther out, where the water swirled and currents struck the perimeter creating breakers but never dislodging the swirl, had been bothering him. When the sea was less boisterous, he saw clearly the many objects trapped in the whorl. Sometimes he found himself gazing, gazing at it, as though it were a covered mirror to be uncovered to reveal the truth about his self. Sometimes he thought the mirror unveiled and he saw himself and his children all trapped in the whirlpool.

He turned away from the sea and looked at his watch. In ten minutes Freddy should be here. He must not call him *young man.* How old was Freddy? He situated the birthdates of two of his children, one in wedlock one out, and figured that Freddy was thirty-eight.

He heard the footsteps on the wooden stairs. Then the knock at the door. Freddy stood in the doorway. He wore leaf-brown slacks and a beige short-sleeved shirt. A slight bulge drew attention to his stomach. More than a sprinkling of grey in his hair. Bushy beard, in places completely white. His piercing eyes and pouting mouth silently asked, *Why did you ask me to come here?*

They greeted each other.

The headmaster scrutinized Freddy, looking for the face and form he remembered. A permanent V marked the spot where his brow used to furrow each time he was disappointed or in deep concentration. The roundness had left his face. It now seemed more angular. The muscles taut. A deep wrinkle was linked to smaller ones under each eye. He had forgotten that Freddy was a Carib. How could he?

"Don't you ever forget that you are a Carib!" Why did I say that to

him? Why did I . . .

"May I sit down?"

"Yes, yes. I didn't intend to keep you standing."

Freddy sat in one of the Morris chairs placed at angles in two corners of the living room and some distance from an oval coffee table in the middle of the living room. The headmaster sat on a two-seater placed against a dividing wall on which there hung an almanac-type print of *The Last Supper*. It rattled slightly each time the breeze gusted. On the street side of the living room there hung from ceiling to floor dirty white curtains which the breeze blew in and out of the windows.

Freddy stared out the seaward window as though he were concentrating on the sound of the waves followed by the seaward drag of the pebbles in concert with the rustling blades of the palm fronds. The light in the room decreased and increased, patterning the outdoor clouding and unclouding of the sun.

"Let me offer you a drink," the headmaster said. "Your silence makes me uncomfortable."

"Thanks. I don't drink." After a pause, "These waves must keep you awake at night. Up the coast where I grew up, they're gentler."

"They don't. But I can't get used to the fury of the sea."

Freddy smiled.

A constant, creaking sound came from the two-seater on which the headmaster sat. He stood up. "I don't know about you, but I need a drink." He walked onto the seaward balcony—some of the lattice work that enclosed it was visible—and turned left. He returned with a twelve-ounce tumbler filled to the brim with ice cubes and rum.

"Since my wife left me, this has been my comfort and solace." He spread his free hand out as he said it. He placed the tumbler on the coffee table, pulled the table near to the two-seater, and resumed his seat. He continued to examine Freddy's face for a reaction.

"You still can't speak. You haven't said two words since you got here."

"I spoke about the sea."

"The sea! To hell with the sea! Talk about people."

Freddy smiled, creasing his cheeks and puckering the outer corners of his eyes. "Why did you invite me here?"

The headmaster fidgeted, stared at the floor, out the seaward window, and again at the floor before looking fixedly ahead of him. He took a deep swallow of rum. "Do you *really* want to know?"

"Not unless you want to tell me."

"I don't like your answer." He got up, walked towards the street window, then turned around to face Freddy. He bent his head a little and began rubbing and rapidly closing his eyes as if trying to recover his sight after a sudden, blinding glare. "You remember your old school well?"

"Yes."

"Where was my office located?"

"Where the walkway ended and the building began. There was a large cedar desk in it and a storeroom was at the back."

The headmaster nodded and returned to his seat.

"How do you find France?"

"Okay."

"Any problems with prejudice?"

"Yes. There, here, everywhere—wherever there are humans."

The headmaster frowned and bit his lower lip. "I've read both of your novels. I heard one of your short stories on Radio Isabella. I like your works. Good stuff. I should've been a writer."

"You'd have probably made a good one."

The conversation lulled again.

"Writing can be very destructive," Freddy said, breaking the silence. "It forces you to expose parts of yourself you prefer to keep hidden."

"That's why I dabbled in it," the headmaster said. "I wrote a few plays but I don't think they were worth much. The kind of stuff to make people laugh, you know."

"At themselves, I hope."

The headmaster sat upright. "You *never* laughed a lot."

Silence. The waves. The wind. The engine of a passing car. The ice cubes in the headmaster's glass.

"You remember your year in my class?"

"Not very well."

"YOU ARE LYING!"

Freddy startled, stared intensely at the headmaster.

"Why don't you tell me," the headmaster asked, his voice languid, "about André, who sat beside you, and pissed down the class the day after I finished beating him? He was Carib too. Like you. WHY DID YOU ALL SIT THERE AND DO NOTHING?"

Freddy's hands went to his ears to muffle the scream.

"Why am I asking you this?" The voice was weary. He emptied his glass in one large swallow. "Do you remember Caroline?"

"Freddy nodded.

"Remember how she died?"

"Yes, she had begun to stink."

"Yes," the headmaster answered drily. "I was the father of that child. . . Aren't you going to say something?"

Freddy stared at him.

"Open your fucking mouth, for Christ sake! . . . Sorry."

Silence.

"I didn't tell her to abort and kill herself. I didn't. I didn't . . . She wasn't quite fourteen."

Silence.

"Listen, I don't like suffering anymore than you do. Your body compels you. Makes you do what you do. Can't blame me for that.

Understand?" He turned his head away from Freddy.

For a while they listened to the sounds of the sea.

The headmaster's mind went back to the school. *Tiny classroom. Long benches. Four to a bench. Clothes filthy. Patches in trousers. Uncombed hair. Ink all over his shirt. Lice. Filthy. Girly antics. Piping voice. Had brains. Definitely had brains. Enter him for a scholarship? Never! Take up valuable space. Keep them in the arrowroot fields. Better off in the fishing canoes. Talking about sex. "Paulus, Stilford, Freddy, come up to the front of the class. What do you know about it? Paulus, stretch out your hand"—one, two, three straps. "Stilford your turn"—one, two, three straps. "Freddy, bend over that desk . . . Completely!" One, two, three, four, five, six. Solid on his back. Blood staining his shirt. Shouldn't have beaten him so hard . . . Why did I hate him?*

"Do your hands still perspire?"

Freddy nodded and looked at his hands. They were perspiring. He held them up for the headmaster to see.

"Why did you always tremble like that?"

Freddy didn't answer.

"You write like someone who understands suffering. You show a lot of sympathy for your characters, even the villains. How come you write like that?"

"I don't know. I suspect that most people are unhappy and try to convince themselves they're not. I deal with such characters." He paused for a while and looked directly ahead of him, as if trying to compose his thoughts. "Unhappiness. It's what religion, philosophy—even prejudice—are all about."

The headmaster got up and headed to the kitchen.

He returned with the tumbler full of rum. He didn't bother with any ice cubes this time. He took a mouthful, then a cigarette pack from his pocket, extracted a cigarette, lit it with trembling fingers, and watched the smoke curl up in the brief intervals when the sea breeze didn't instantly disperse it. He returned to the kitchen for an ash tray. As he stubbed out the cigarette, he muttered, "So you don't think I'm a murderer." He paused, began to reach for the cigarette pack on the coffee table but changed his mind. "I'm sixty-seven, you know." His tone was plaintive, regretful. "The corn's been harvested. Stubble's all that's left."

Silence.

The headmaster broke it, mumbling to himself inaudibly. He stared at the billowing curtains. He turned and faced Freddy. "Tell me something: why are humans so putrid? So small?" To himself he muttered, "Putrid and small. Empty except when full o' shit. Why?" He stared now into Freddy's eyes. "ANSWER ME!" His face contorted, he compressed his lips and shook his fists. "YOU SHOULD KNOW! YOU MUST KNOW! YOU ARE A WRITER! . . . Pardon me. No reason to lose my temper like this." He stopped, seemed to be having an epiphany, then resumed. "No, 1 mustn't be angry with you. I mustn't be. I mustn't. OH GOD! I mustn't." He shivered, shaking his head, arms, and entire torso. Agony was visible in every part of his body.

A long pause followed. He took a few gulps of rum and closed his eyes for short periods. When he resumed speaking his eyes were closed. "I should've done like you. These hundred and seventy square miles, almost all mountains, is the only world I know."

Another long pause.

"Last year, they honoured me with an MBE. Gave it to me, the sons-o-bitches, because they never promoted me. While speaker after speaker spewed shit, I felt like going up on that podium and screaming out to them how many schoolgirls I'd slept with. They couldn't have done a damn thing; I'd already retired. Come to think of it, the goddamn buzzards might've invited me to do it with their wives. It's rumoured that the education officer—oh, never mind him . . . "

The rum was disappearing fast from the tumbler. The headmaster emptied the last few drops, and as he rose to go to the kitchen, he asked, "What is man? What is man, really though?"

He returned with a full bottle of rum. He had left the tumbler in the kitchen. He did not sit down immediately. He swayed perilously. "Look out there," he said, indicating the whirlpool about fifty metres from the shore.

Freddy got up and looked.

"All of us are in it! Every last one!"

Freddy nodded.

"DON'T THINK BECAUSE YOU'RE A WRITER YOU'RE NOT IN IT. YOU HEAR? Pardon me." He was swaying more now. "We're all in it," he repeated in a whisper, as he swayed to the two-seater and sat down heavily. He brought the bottle to his lips and gulped. He put it down on the coffee table, noisily. "My wife—married her when she was fourteen . . . father would o' killed me if I didn't . . . damn fool I was . . . bred her and married her . . . gave me four children . . . aborted two . . . left me . . . sleeping with everybody in New York . . . I hear." In an apologetic tone, he added, "I'm too hard on her. Too hard. I was no saint." He picked up the bottle. "Good medicine this. Have one. Oh I forgot: Freddy the saint doesn't drink. Freddy the saint can write. Can Freddy the saint fuck? Doesn't drink. TOO GODDAMN IMPORTANT TO DRINK! Can never be too important to fuck. I always thought you were gay. Maybe that was why. . ." He gulped long and hard.

He held on to the bottle and began to squint as if he were seeing Freddy through fog. "Boy, I have a question to ask you: How your name got on the scholarship list?"

Freddy didn't answer.

"Boy, why you don' answer me? In the good ol' days I wouldo' whale yo' arse good and proper." He took another gulp. "Caroline ever give you any? It didn' have any blood on she clothes when I take the piece. Her death teach me a lesson. Boy, French women ever blow you? I hear they the best in the world. Naw, with you I sure is French men. Boy, how come your name got on the scholarship list? I never put it there? Was Paulus's name alone I write. He wouldn't o' get it though. I never sen' yo' name in. After you got that scholarship I wondered day and night if I was crazy. Did a spell come over me and I put your name on that form too and didn' remember? Did I drink too much that day and didn' remember what I did? Boy, when you got that scholarship I almost went crazy. I did promise Paulus father faithfully to put down Paulus name only." He took another draught from the bottle.

"You remember Paulus? Father had the big rum shop by the cross-road? Boy, you cause me to lose free rum. Couldn't face the man after yo' name come out. Call me serpent. Say I drink he rum for free and deceive he. I couldn' even tell the sonofabitch wasn' me that sen' yo' name in." He was swaying heavily in the two-seater and his speech was thick; his lungs rattled slightly. "You ever betray yourself? . . been a traitor to yourself?" His head bobbed as if he'd been suddenly dozing and waking up. "Annuder thing. . . I hear writers—artists— love kinky sex." He tried to do the broken-wing gesture homophobes use, but the rum in his system defeated him. He steadied himself as much as he could, focused on the rum bottle, grabbed it, and cradled it to his chest with both arms. "I always wanted to know what it feel like for a man to fuck me—all my life—ain't never had the courage. . . Think you can oblige me? . . . Go to hell. Can't even bull!" He was rocking from front to back and side to side now, hitting the back of the two-seater and bouncing forward. The rum bottle fell from his clasp and crashed. "Wha' fell?" He leaned forward and keeled over into the pieces of broken bottle, struck the coffee table on its edge and knocked it onto its side.

Freddy went to the toilet. When he returned the headmaster's head lay in a puddle of vomit. Some of it was still trickling down the corner of his mouth. Freddy took a small notepad and a pen from the pocket of his shirt. He wrote:

Martha James, your assistant, went into your office one day and saw the scholarship form on your desk and the addressed envelope. She knew that my name should have been on the list, so she added it and sealed the envelope. She told me to go and write the exam but I was not to tell anyone. It wasn't until I finished high school that she told me the entire story.

On the subject of which of your acts you're responsible for I cannot help you. I'd like to say, stay away from the bottle, but perhaps you cannot, not before you resolve what sends you to seek refuge in it.

He went to the kitchen and took one of the empty rum bottles on the counter and used it as a paper weight to prevent the wind from blowing away the note. He returned to the living room and took one more look at the headmaster. He was mumbling incoherently to himself. Flies had begun to congregate on him.

Emory

JOE PUSHES THE WHEELCHAIR. Harriet brings along the IV pole. They settle Emory in a sheltered corner of the balcony away from the sun's reach. Harriet attaches the beeper to the wheelchair. There's no need to tell Emory, "Press it once for pain; twice if you think you need oxygen; three if you need to go to the bathroom." Harriet spreads a blanket across the armrests of the wheelchair, and asks him if he is comfortable. He nods. She and Joe return inside.

Days like today Emory likes being out here. The sky is cloudless and the breeze gentle. Every few seconds, plovers—white, their wings extended or flapping—skim over the sea and occasionally dive into it. His eyes dart over the different hues of the Caribbean Sea—oval blue, emerald, turquoise, here and there flecked with foam from the gently breaking waves. He listens to the surf's lapping: a mother singing sort of, a mother humming a lullaby to her child, the shore, a hundred metres below, down the steep slope under the balcony of The Tranquillity Convalescent Home. And there's the faint smell—the sea's smell— living, indefinable, barely perceptible, like a human body's. Yesterday, rain and a howling wind kept him inside. The mother whipping her child. Opposite states of nature that used to make him sigh and sometimes shrug. Opposite states of nature that helped him, eventually, explain his own cruelty and kindness. Days like yesterday, he stays in his room hooked up to oxygen, and listens to the roiling sea and the angry wind hissing off it. And doesn't get the peace he relies on during the day to help him withstand the horrors of the night.

Occasionally the horrors visit him during the day—always when he's in his room. Not that the room's a bad one. It's big enough; is air-conditioned; has a comfortable, mechanically adjustable bed, he simply has to press a button; ample closet space; a comfortable recliner right beside a bay window with a view of the sea and the blue-grey forms of the Dependencies in the distance. On occasion he sees and hears the planes ascending or descending as they take off or land at the airport in the valley a mile behind the hill.

This place is one of two achievements Emory is proud of. He'd got the idea when he was a young policeman, nineteen, just out of training, that policemen should pool their meagre savings for their mutual benefit. He'd heard a radio documentary about the credit union movement in Canada, and he thought something like that would be good for police officers. But the island's major bank had bribed the upper echelons in the force not to move on it, and nothing came of his proposal, until Emory himself became part of the upper echelon. By then too the teachers had created their credit union, so had the civil servants, and Emory was able to shame his colleagues into seeing that if they had taken up his idea twenty years earlier, they would have pioneered the credit union movement on Isabella Island. He always looked for opportunities to be innovative. And his wife Adelle had always encouraged his forays of this sort. Rather than have all that cash on hand, he told her, they should put it into valuable services, and she'd agreed and told him to keep on pushing.

He'd grown up beside the sea, in a remote part of the Leeward Coast, and all his life he had loved its tranquility, though he knows many who think that the sound of waves lapping or pounding the shore is anything but tranquil. Many times he'd driven above the spot where he is now hospitalized and wondered who owned it. It would be great for a hotel he'd thought: a four-or five-star hotel. Isabella Island was a developing tourist economy. He told himself several times that he'd go to the Registry to find out its owner, but never got around to it. In the meantime, he goaded his colleagues on the credit union board to look out for opportunities to invest in the burgeoning tourist industry, and they got involved in a couple of ventures in the Grenadines.

One Saturday morning he was lazily flipping the pages of *The Isabellan* when an article about the lack of convalescent facilities on the island caught his attention. A half dozen people who'd sought respite from looking after their very ill relatives could find none and had expressed some unprintable words, the reporter said, about how backward Isabella Island was. It was then that the idea came to Emory. Three days later, while driving on the slope above this spot, he saw a for sale sign—for two and three-quarter acres all the way down to the sea. Within the hour, he called up the realtor and the CU board members. They were unimpressed. Emory, who'd been investing in the American stock market, knew a thing or two about why medical stocks were high. Within weeks he convinced his colleagues that the many emigrants returning from England, the United States, and Canada to retire invariably left their children behind but brought along fat health insurance policies and fatter bank accounts and would need convalescent services soon. He brought on board the two members who were still opposed, when he proposed that ailing police officers or their spouses should have priority places in the facility and pay only a tiny fraction of the cost. Initially they'd planned for six rooms. There was a waiting list even before the facilities were completed, so they redrew the plans and enlarged it to twelve. Four luxury rooms on the seaward side, like the one Emory now occupies, were created specially for police officers and their relatives. These, when no police or family member needed them, were to be rented out at luxury rates, on the understanding that if they were required the occupants would be moved to less appointed facilities. That was fifteen years ago. The long waiting list resulted in the Police CU building another, more modest, facility; the teachers' CU and the civil servants' CU followed suit with one each. All of them had waiting lists. Three years ago, when the latest facility was opened, a journalist for *The Isabellan* had written a piece praising Emory for his vision and his service to the police "brotherhood" and Isabellans on the whole. But not everyone held the same view of Emory.

He looks out over the sea. Recessed in the corner of the balcony, he's unable to see the shoreline. He'd like to. There'd be people walking along it. Something about walking along the black sand, the land to his left, the mountains towering just a short distance away, sometimes cloud-capped, the sea on his right: the solid and the liquid, the ever-moving line between blue sea and black land, the force of the sea that always made him think it was a living thing, a gigantic maw that was forever trying to swallow the earth, the way he'd learned that some snakes engulf their prey . . . He was not afraid of snakes and he was not afraid of the sea.

Adelina, his daughter, a surgeon in Daytona Beach, Florida, would be arriving today. His and Adelle's only child. Adelle was 19 years old and a nursing student in her second year, and he not quite twenty-one, when they'd met and she'd got pregnant. With a little prodding from his mother he'd done the honourable thing. That's

his second accomplishment: his family. His colleagues never understood him. Most had trouble juggling their schedules to keep up
with the girlfriends they had in the various villages they'd worked
in. "You live only once, Emory. Get all the fun you can." He never
saw the fun. His colleagues, those who supported the children
resulting from such relationships, the few who did, were always
broke. And if they managed to have a decent home, it was because
of their wives, who were usually teachers, or nurses, or civil servants. Some of his colleagues took their needs beyond legal limits,
and Emory, in the years when he was a station sergeant, was forced
on more than one occasion to bungle the evidence to keep charges
from being brought. Where the mothers held out—with such young
women fathers were never in the picture—he'd get his subordinates
to pay hush money after convincing the mothers that it would not be
such a good thing to have their daughters' names besmirched by the
dirt a trial would dish up. Mothers are an understanding lot. They
know how the real world works. When Master Billy, the grandson of
Pleasant Pastures' proprietor, had raped Muriel, Emory's sister, and
Emory's uncle threatened to bring in the law, their mother reasoned
with him. Old man Laird, Billy's father, had offered her two hundred
dollars to keep the matter quiet. Eventually Uncle saw reason—after
all they were squatters on Old Man Laird's plantation—and got Old
Man Laird to up the figure to three hundred. Emory did not see it
their way then. He would have killed Billy then if it had been left up
to him.

Emory sighs. "The fathers eat the sour grapes and the children's
teeth are set on edge." A sensible biblical statement. One of the few
he finds useful. "The sins of the fathers are visited upon the children." He hopes that's not always true. Pleasant Pastures Estates; his
beginning; his undoing; the arrowroot field; Laird's overseer cheating his mother and the other workers as he measured the arrowroot

they'd dug—a Black man cheating Blacks for a few extra cents of pay. The world turns on power. Power procures wealth. Power preserves wealth. Power protects. Power. Power.

Emory is proud, proud that he never cheated on his wife, proud that he never had a bevy of mistresses on whom to splurge his earnings. Proud of his daughter. That part of his life has been a success: his most important achievement. Would his daughter be proud of him?

Not so proud of other things. Not so proud. *"The fathers eat the sour grapes . . . "* They do. Billy Laird, they do. Adelle on her deathbed. In one of these same rooms. Dying from uraemia. Her bloated body hooked up to the dialysis machine. "Emory, did you kill Billy?" He was too surprised to answer. "The truth, Emory." He shook his head, meaning to say, or so he thought then, we shouldn't be talking about this. She squeezed his hand, and her face relaxed. Now *he* has at the most three months to live, and has come here to spend them, and he can no longer lie to himself. He deceived her in death. She'd asked for the truth and he'd withheld it. And it's a blot on the perfect marriage that he sees as his second achievement.

Helena and Dorothy, girlfriends of the two other police officers, and Adelle never wavered in their belief that Emory, Michael, and Zachariah were innocent. He'd never suspected that Adelle ever doubted his version of the facts. To cover up the occasional nightmares he had been having about the second victim—not about Billy, he deserved what he got—he'd prepared a strategy to counter doubts that might have arisen. He'd have told her that one of Laird's cronies owned *The Isabellan* and had used it to spread propaganda against him and his colleagues. One week there was certainly the piece in the paper about the crucial witness who had seen it all and would come forward with evidence. A piece the next week claimed that the witness had drowned in questionable circumstances. It was normal that *The Isabellan*, owned by the Pembertons, Laird's cronies, would report that the police had drowned the witness.

Pain shoots from Emory's groin and spreads out over his lower back and abdomen. He presses the beeper. Harriet comes with a syringe and injects morphine into the IV. She asks him if he wants to go inside. He shakes his head.

"Mr. Bowles!" Emory opens his eyes, rubs them, and sees the two women standing with their backs to the sea. Almost instantly Adelina bends down to kiss and embrace him.

"I'm so glad you've come," he tells her as he struggles to remove the blanket to put his arms around her.

Adelina releases him, removes the blanket, then kneels, and they embrace properly.

Emory cries.

Adelina's eyes well up but do not spill. "Papa, how are you bearing up?"

"As good as I can. As good as I can, my dear child." He pauses for breath. "As good as I can."

"I see you have trouble sleeping. I came in about fifteen minutes ago and saw that you were sleeping. So I took the time to see what's been written in your chart since the two weeks I was here."

Emory says nothing. He stares at his daughter, still youthful looking at 47. She is dark brown like Adelle, but has his oval features and the aquiline nose he inherited from his plantation grandfather, who never acknowledged Emory's father—Emory's father was Billy's Laird's cousin—who in turn never acknowledged Emory. Adelina's streamlined body is also from him. He's happy to see her. Occasions like these tell him that, gossip or not, the family bond holds. "Let's go inside, so we can talk private." He beeps, and Joe comes and pushes the wheelchair inside. Adelina brings along the IV pole.

Joe puts him in the recliner. Emory shakes his head when he's offered oxygen. Adelina sits on the foot of the bed. The sun is streaming into the window from across the Caribbean Sea. She gets up, closes the blinds, presses the remote for the air conditioner, and returns to sit at the foot of the bed.

"So what are we going to do about your sleeping problem?"

Emory says nothing.

"I'll speak to Dr. Galloway to see if we can increase the sedation. How are you managing with pain control?"

With headshakes he gestures half-and-half.

"You only have to let the staff know. You know that. You're to have as much morphine as you need."

He nods. He'd rather hear her talk about her life. She's always been taciturn. As far as he knows she's single. They've never had a conversation about children. She's usually off here and there taking or giving courses, honing up on something or other, imparting skills to others, picking up skills from others—all over the place. She's won so many awards, he cannot count them. Did medicine at Yale. Never cost him a cent. And Emory is proud: he had produced her—he, whose mother could not afford to send him to a secondary school and was never able to give him and Muriel enough to eat. He too hadn't done too badly either. He rose to number three in command of the Isabellan Police Force.

He and Adelina are silent. Harriet comes, replaces the almost empty IV sac, asks again if he needs oxygen. He shakes his head. She leaves. Emory wonders if he should turn over the document he has prepared for Adelina. He looks at her. She's staring vacantly out the bay window. The document's in a sealed envelope in his night table. No, when he's sure the end is near. His earlier decision was rash.

He thinks of what he has written. Tells himself that what we want is never fully what we get, and we're lucky if we get a part of what we want. What does he want? For her to know the truth. Why? He knows that he knows why but something prevents him from putting it into words. "Adelina."

She turns and gives him her full attention.

He says nothing.

"What is it, Papa?"

"Oh, I don't know. It's so silent. Guess I'm seeing whether I'm still alive. Turn that air conditioner off, dear." That's not really what he wanted to say. He wants to tell her why he cannot sleep, why every time he falls asleep he feels someone tickling his jaws and awakens to see Billy Laird, brain marrow oozing from his forehead, standing at his bedside.

He'd thought that the other death would have bothered him more. During the trial it did. When Emory became third in command and in charge of complaints against police officers, Bailey, then commissioner of police, told him he'd recommended him for promotion because he needed someone in that position who'd be cooperative. He wonders whether he'd have accepted the posting if he'd known Bailey's intention. Earlier in Bailey's career, when he was in charge of investigations, he'd done Emory and his colleagues a great favour. Now Bailey was collecting. He promised Emory that he'd be handsomely rewarded for his cooperation, and he was. Thereafter Emory paid all his bills with cash and invested his and Adelle's entire salary. He never let Adelle in on what he was doing. He continued to drive his old car and to live in their modest bungalow. Too many of his colleagues had given away their game by spending more than their salaries could pay for. Bailey gave him a list of people, drug lords mostly, that he was protecting, and Emory's job was to ensure that no investigations were done on them. He was to prosecute, even persecute, their competitors vigorously, and when members of the competition were killed, he was to make sure the investigation trails go cold. Bailey assured him that he had his back covered and had a muzzle for every possible squealer. Eventually, Emory shrugged his shoulders, mused that he hadn't created the world; his duty was to survive in it. He was sure that's what Commissioner Bain would have told him if he were still around. He convinced himself that if he hadn't been born poor he'd have had other choices. You play with the hand life dealt you; you make sure you get the stakes and aren't the stake.

"Billy Laird," he says out loud.

"What, Papa. What did you say?"

Emory shakes his head.

"Are you alright?"

He nods.

The fateful night it had been Emory's turn to ticket reckless drivers on a dangerous stretch of road on the Windward Highway—a job assigned to rookie cops. Billy Laird, around thirty then, a wastrel, drunk, and wencher, came zooming down the stretch. Emory stopped the red corvette. Billy stared into Emory's face, recognized him, spat, and gunned his motor, leaving Emory standing by the side of the road. Emory alerted his colleagues and joined them about three miles down the road. They already had handcuffs on Billy when Emory arrived. In a daze, Emory went at him with his truncheon. By the time Emory's colleagues restrained him, Billy's skull had been crushed. They looked at one another, nodded, threw Billy's limp body into the jeep, drove to the edge of the nearby promontory, and threw the body over the cliff with the handcuffs still on. Michael had to walk two miles around the promontory to remove the handcuffs. They reported that Billy had resisted arrest, bolted from them, run to the precipice, and jumped over.

The coroner, a leftover from colonial times, felt otherwise, and hence the trial. A young fisherman lived on the bank above where the beating had taken place, and he'd witnessed it. Bailey, then in charge of complaints against police officers, kept the fisherman under surveillance. He drowned two days after Laird's solicitor was seen coming from his house. An accident at sea. The details were kept from Emory. After six months of paid suspension, a judge dismissed the case against Emory and his colleagues for want of evidence.

A week after the not-guilty verdict, two weeks after May Day 1969, and a week after Emory's twenty-second birthday, Commissioner Bain, the last pre-Independence British appointee to hold the job, met with the three of them the day they were reinstated. They stood facing his desk, their backs to the window that fronted the courtyard. Bain was seated, and for a long time he stared down at the empty, glowing surface of his mahogany desk. When he raised his head he gave each of them, an intense stare, his eyes moving from right to left. He spoke then. "You will find . . . " He stopped, stared down at the surface of his desk, and didn't finish that sentence. He began again. "Everything you've learned in church and Sunday school teaches you that if you take a human life, you should be punished for it." He paused. "It's piffle. Dismiss it. I was a conscript in World War II. Got wounded too. They sent me to shed blood. They told me to save my life but take the enemy's. I'm not responsible for the lives I took in war and a few more since putting on this uniform." He paused again, a little longer. "Let society be responsible." He stopped talking, looked up at the ceiling, and repeated the right to left stare. He was a man of massive build, more than six feet, around sixty; had thin auburn hair, round jowly features, and blue, deep-set eyes that looked kind when he was relaxed and cruel when he was not.

"Ours is a thankless job. Society despises us for doing it. We make mistakes, serious mistakes sometimes. But it comes with the territory. It's all in a day's work. Don't lose sleep over it, mates, don't yer do it." He kept them standing there for another five minutes without saying anything, then he got up, walked around his desk to them, and shook their hands. Now recalling this, Emory remembers that in those days no one had heard about the Geneva Convention. He remembers laughing when he found out about it. How foolish could human beings get? Rules for the conduct of war! The first and only clause in that convention should be indefinite incarceration for the head of state whose behaviour threatens war, or has the audacity to begin war.

For a long time afterwards Emory consoled himself with the thought that he'd killed Billy, albeit unintentionally, because Laird's ilk needed to know independence had come, and things had changed on Isabella Island. Blacks would no longer be the playthings of the wealthy Whites, or bow their heads and swallow and cry when they were raped, exploited, and dissed. Even now it astonishes him how fully Commissioner Bain had cooperated. Five years earlier, the judge who tried Emory and his colleagues would have been White, and would have found a way to avenge Billy Laird's death. Quite likely all three of them would have been hanged; at the very least they'd have got long prison sentences.

He sighs out loud. He was sorry about the drowned fellow though. He wished it could have been avoided. It was only when he came to put it all down on paper for Adelina's benefit that he understood that he'd made Billy Laird pay for what had been done to Emory's paternal grandmother and what Billy himself had done to Muriel. *The sins of the fathers. . .* But the fisherman, whose name he hasn't remembered . . . Collateral damage. How do soldiers, soldiers of fortune especially, and professional assassins do it and lead normal lives? Does his colleague—he doesn't know which one—who dispatched the fisherman have nightmares? All he knows is that he was someone in charge of explosives. Commissioner Bain had lied to them, Emory now knows, but it was a necessary lie. Maybe, when all's said and done, the truth does set us free.

A week ago when Muriel visited him, she brought him six mangoes in a plastic bag, and cowheel soup in a plastic container. She'd used an elastic band to secure the cover further. He saw the usefulness of the plastic bag and the rubber band and kept them. Two days later, on the phone with Adelina, he told her there was something he wanted to settle with her. After speaking, he realized he had been reckless. Now here she is.

He looks up at Adelina sitting at the foot of the bed. "I'm tired. Come early tomorrow morning for the instructions I have for you." He beeps.

Harriet and Joe come. He tells them to help him into bed.

Adelina bends over and kisses him. "I'll see you tomorrow, Papa." She hesitates at the door, spends a full minute staring at him, before she exits.

Fifteen minutes later he beeps. "The pain's unbearable," he tells Harriet. "Let me have the morphine dispenser."

She connects it to the valve lower down on the IV. He tells her not to turn it on. She shows him again how to operate it and leaves. He'll wait until they've changed shifts. With his free hand, he reaches into the night table, takes out the plastic bag and elastic band and does a dry run. No problem. *The sins of the fathers . . .* It's time to bequeath his to the next generation. A wave of relaxation moves through him as he thinks that he'll sleep tonight and never have to worry about tomorrow.

Garifuna

IT'S FEBRUARY 17, 2011, and I'm sitting under a coconut tree on the beach that runs the length of Hopkins Village, Belize. It's damn cold in Montreal, and so you'd think I'm here to soak up the sun and loll on this multi-mile beach. Believe me, the golden sand, turquoise water, and gentle waves are alluring: irresistible. But it's not why I'm here.

My thoughts turn to my grandmother and her sister, my great-aunt Aggie. Grama did not speak to her and forbade me from telling anyone that she was my aunt. Both had partly fibrous hair—Grama wore hers in two braids—and honey-coloured skin. These traits, Grama said, were from their Carib ancestors: the indigenous people of Isabella Island, St Vincent, and most of the islands of the Lesser Antilles. Grama had come from St Vincent to live on Isabella Island following her marriage to Grandad, whose surname Summerville was also the name of our village. It had been founded by his fore-bears, who'd fought the Black Caribs (Kalinago) for almost a century and eventually expelled them and seized their lands. Aggie had come to Isabella too, to become Bozo's common-law wife. She was fifteen years younger than Grama, one of the rare bits of information I got out of her. Our relatives visiting from St Vincent avoided her too. Grama's curt explanation was: "She disgraced us" (something she also said about my mother). Obeah was a word that frightened us, and Aunt Aggie's common-law husband was a famous—or infamous, depending on one's class—obeahman. I assumed that was the reason why Grama and our Vincentian relatives had ostracized her.

I pestered Grama with questions about the Caribs. She didn't answer them and said I shouldn't bother her with old-time stories. I'd stare into her amber eyes and feel my frustration grow. By the time I had some of the answers and might have shared them with her, she could not remember what she'd had for breakfast, and her eyes lay under a milky blue film.

Grama has been dead for more than forty years, but in recent years I have found myself going to Central America regularly, and it's only now, having just listened to Mr Coley, that I realize that these trips that have taken me to Livingston in Guatemala, Bluefield, Marshall Point, and Oronoco in Nicaragua, and now to Punta Gorda, Dangriga, and Hopkins Village in Belize—all Garifuna towns and villages—are in some way connected to the don't-bother-me responses I got from Grama when I questioned her about her Kalinago ancestry. (In university I found out that Carib was a name Columbus imposed on the Kalinago for his own peculiar purposes.) I'll have to make a trip to Dominica too. A French priest wrote about the seventeenth-century Kalinago—he uses the word—in nearby Guadeloupe. I wonder if Dominicans know. The Central Americans don't. Would be a good opportunity for them to find out.

Aunt Aggie went mad. I was present the night it happened. My mother, who lived in New York, visited us on average every two years, and on one of those visits, the year before I began university in Jamaica, we defied Grama and visited Aggie at the Good Shepherd Mental Asylum. We found her sitting on the floor of the ward, muttering to herself. She did not speak to us. I doubt she knew who we were.

The catalytic event took place on a Saturday when I was sixteen and in the first term of GCE A-level classes: forty-eight years ago. It rained all that day. I'm pretty sure it was late November. Around noon a neighbour shouted through the drizzle and across the fence to Grama: "Dorothy, if this rain don't stop, they will have to cancel the rejoicing tonight."

"What rejoicing? Didn't you tell me Aggie didn't get clearance?" Grama said, pausing from the dough she was kneading and staring out the kitchen window across at the neighbour.

Edith replied, "That is what I heard. I don't understand why they going through with this . . . All this bad weather. You think is Bozo that cause all this rain? Dorothy, he's a powerful obeahman."

"Edith, you and your foolishness. That man is a fraud," Grama said.

Bozo was reputed to have helped several women recapture their husbands from mistresses. Edith's husband Hilton had returned to her after living five years with a mistress. Had Bozo helped her?

Just before five the rain stopped suddenly, and the skies cleared, and the wind dropped to a very light breeze. The Anglican Church bell had just tolled six and the darkness was intensifying quickly. Water drops on the tree leaves reflected the light from a two-thirds full moon.

Summerville is on a plateau one quarter of the way up a steep mountain, at the foot of which is gently sloping land that goes all the way to the sea. We watched the procession from two kilometres away, down in the bottom of the valley, making its way on the road which closely follows the meandering river.

The believers, in white, each carrying a lighted candle, looked like saints on their way to the eschatological rendezvous. *That's how Grama would have put it.* The martial strains of "Onward Christian Soldiers" suffused the valley and wafted up the slope of the mountain. I was at the Lookout. It was crowded, but more people were coming and jostling those already there to get a better view.

The procession drew closer, and now I could discern the sashes, surplices, and headgear that denoted rank, all of it decorating the head of what looked like a white, glowing, massive candle-studded snake tunneling through the darkness and ascending toward the village. The three leaders and Sister Aggie were separated from the others by about two metres. Pointer Lumley—his purple surplice unmistakable—was at the front; half a metre behind were Sister Aggie and Mother Biddy; behind them, about a half metre, was Bishop "Breeder." Positioned thus the four formed the shape of a cross; and, because of the distance between them and the rest of the Believers, the procession also looked like a severed body following after its head.

Now the Lookout was packed and latecomers were looking for places on other ledges. Some of the young people were on rooftops. The few houses with upstairs balconies were crowded.

To my right, about ten metres away, was a broad expanse of land that was the village common. It was where most outdoor activities took place: the moonlight dances, the mock hangings, the cricket matches, revival meetings . . . I was distracted by a bright light moving towards it, and discerned Harry, holding a Coleman lamp, his nephew, Gad, a lad around fifteen, and Beryl, who held a shopping bag, all three dressed in white. They set up a light pole and hung the lamp onto it, arranged a small circular table beside it, and placed a vase of white river lilies and four lit candles on the table. The light shone all the way to Father Flattelley's porch. He was sitting there observing them, but now he got up and headed indoors. He was the Anglican priest for nearby Camden, but he'd chosen to live in Summerville. Like Grama and a few other villagers—the Summerville bourgeoisie—he held the Believers in contempt. The tasks of the three now completed, they faced the candles, crossed themselves, bowed their heads in unison, and retreated without ever turning their backs until they were outside the circle of light.

By now the head of the procession had arrived at the steep ascent leading up to Summerville, about a hundred metres from the gathering place. I imagine that if this had been a Garifuna event they'd have entered to the sounds of drumming. In Africa, there would have been drums too. The singing stopped. At intervals a bell rang. That was Bishop Breeder's office. Pointer Lumley told me the ringing bell was to summon the ancestral spirits. The procession was now entering the village, and the participating societies were unfurling their banners. The first, right after the head had passed, was HOLY AFRICAN BELIEVERS OF ASHBY, followed by HOLY AFRICAN BELIEVERS OF BERLIN . . . The head of the procession—comprising Mother Biddy, Sister Aggie (she was blindfolded), Pointer Lumley, and Bishop Breeder, who was still ringing the hand bell—was now positioned around the table, and around them the Believers were forming circles (the coiling of the luminous serpent: "The Abomey Serpent, Jim. It upholds the cosmos," Pointer Lumley told me once, but refused to say more). Finally all nine societies were in place. There was one last display of their banners before they rolled them up and put them away.

Now the onlookers from all the lookout points were converging on the commons and jostling one another for a better spot. Bishop Breeder cleared a space among them to walk to the rum shop across from the common. Someone came out of it staggering and shouted, "Breeder, which one o' the women-them you going breed tonight?" Breeder's form disappeared into the rum shop and he spent about five minutes in there. He had been a pointer. But a certain young woman gave birth nine months after he'd piloted her. He denied paternity, but his daughter had inherited even Breeder's extra diminutive fingers. Consequently, he had been demoted from Pointer to Bishop, and everyone, including children, began to call him Bishop Breeder. He too was from St Vincent. Grama was his distant cousin. She told me the story of Breeder's demotion, and I have no doubt, it was to discredit the religion.

Bishop Breeder emerged from the rum shop, the drunks staggered out behind him, the lights of the rum shop went out, and the next phase of the ceremony began. Bishop Breeder took the bell and turned to the south and rang it, to the west and rang it, to the north and rang it, and to the east and rang it. Next he kissed the ground. He straightened and made a wide sweep of the hand while looking at Mother Biddy, signalling that he was turning the proceedings over to her. Mother Biddy limped to the light pole. She was afflicted with several leg ulcers, which would heal in one area and then erupt in others. They'd caused her legs to atrophy, but it hadn't affected the swing of her bottom, probably had accented it. She was roseau-thin. "A broomstick," some said.

She was reputed to have prophetic powers. Around 4 AM on Sunday mornings I often heard her proclaiming her latest vision, the surrounding hills echoing every word. Stuff like:

"Children, awake and hearken. Turn from your wicked ways, for the coming of the Lord is nigh. I just had the vision. A man in a white gown and his two hands dripping blood, he come down out of the sky

and say to me, 'My chosen, go and warn them hard-hearted, stiff-neck children of mine to turn from their wicked ways, 'cause I is ready to pour out my wrath on them."

Now Mother Biddy addressed the crowd, "Brothers and sisters, thank you all for joining with us tonight to celebrate this joyful time, a time for us to rejoice, sing hallelujah, and strengthen our faith."

"Amen, Mother," the crowd responded.

"Is a time when we evil deeds purge away, when we come back clean and safe from the valley of death where we done meet our loved ones gone on before, where we done see them face to face, and converse with them, and seek their guidance, and learn their wisdom. Oh friends and Believers, what a blessed time!" Her chest and her bottom swung to the rhythm of her voice. "No sweeter time; none, my children, none."

She began to sing, "My faith looks up to thee." The crowd, picked up the tune, dragging out the syllables. As the first line ended, she lined out the second: "Thou Lamb of Calvary." She was illiterate, but she knew her hymns. The singing thundered through the valley, echoing, and creating its own symphony—or babel for those who felt like Grama and Father Flattelly.

The singing ended and the praying started. Pointer Lumley, with the highest rank, was first to pray: a chant in which the sounds of each line were juggled to peak midway, followed by a pause for an audience response, and it always began with an invocation of the Trinity:

"In the name of God the father."

Amen.

"In the name of God the son."

Amen.

"In the name of God the Holy Ghost."

Amen.

"My sinful knees I bow."

Amen.

"I pray for Sister Aggie."

Amen.

"I pray for her peace of mind."

Amen.

"I pray for all her loved ones."

Amen.

"I pray for all mankind.

Amen.

"Holy Ghost and my redeemer."

Amen.

"Descend on true believers."

"Amen! Amen ! Skatcha! Skatcha!" This from Mother Biddy.

"Amen," spectators and believers shouted with doubled zest.

"Sister, sister, oh Sister Aggie!"

Amen.

"Fill her heart and never leave her."

Amen.

Peace, oh peace, oh peace, oh peace."

Amen.

"Enter and never leave."

Amen.

"Never choose to take release."

Amen.

"Follow her to her decease."

Amen.

"Now I pray for Mother Biddy."

Amen.

Give her strength for her to tarry.

Amen.

"Bring an end to the afflictions of her body."

Amen.

"Lord, we know that she's your vessel.

Amen.

"To carry your truth and prophecy."

Amen.

"Bless her and grant her vision."

Amen.

"To lead forth your chosen children."

Amen.

And thus we continued for another thirty or so minutes.

Pointer Lumley was around sixty: a tiny, short man, barely five feet. But what a voice in that wizened frame! He rarely used its full force. He was probably the only literate member among the three leaders present. Class norms on Isabella Island dictated that he shouldn't belong to the Believers. In our village, he was probably the only person of his generation with a high school diploma. Apart from the two plantocrats with two-thousand-acre plantations to the north and south of us, Lumley, Robertson Bailey—in neighbouring Hillsdale—and Granddad were the only large landholders. Lumley owned about two hundred acres of excellent land, slightly less than Granddad and Mr Bailey but of better quality.

A Sunday morning, a year earlier, just as Grama and I stepped out the door to go to church, he came through our gate and told Grama that he'd received a call from "yonder" for her to get on board the Believers' ship. Grama laughed. "Go'long, Lumley, you just go'long, you hear me. Because they duped you, you now think you can dupe me? I born a Methodist, Lumley. I baptize a Methodist, and I will die a Methodist. Tell that, you hear me, to the man or woman who gave you that message."

"It came from the Holy Ghost, Sister Summerville."

"Don't you sister me, Lumley. I'm not your sister anymore." She wagged a finger at him. "Reverend Wimbleton excommunicated you . . ."

"Twenty-seven years ago."

I liked Pointer Lumley. Grama thought he was a fraud, and those messages he said he got from yonder were his schemes to draw members away from the other churches. I felt otherwise. He'd spent time in prison for belonging to the Believers. Until 1951 his religion and all practices that were thought to have originated in Africa were illegal. It was why there were no drums at tonight's procession. All three leaders there that night had been jailed on various occasions, depending on the whims or ambitions of the police officers assigned to the station in Hillsdale.

Pointer Lumey lived three houses down the road from us. He was single. He had two floor-to-ceiling book cases packed with books, and he was always adding new ones. On the floor beside the bookcases were three piles of newspapers: *The Manchester Guardian*, *The Isabellan*, and *The Informer*. He had more books about Africa— over thirty of them—than in the Hanovertown Public Library. I'd already read a couple of them: one about the Akan concept of God and another about the Kalahari Bushmen. Of course, I'd kept them hidden in my school bag and taken them out only when Grama wasn't around. The only books about Africa she'd have wanted me reading would have been those written by missionaries who'd gone there to rescue Africans from "heathenism." She begged diligently for money to finance those missions. Sitting in his wheelchair, Granddad, who by then was paraplegic, and she sometimes argued over it. I suspect that he was agnostic but could never say more than, "Hester, your God sure keeps you busy." And then he'd wink at me if Grama's back were turned.

Looking back on it now, I can see why she feared that Pointer

Lumley was trying to lure me into his religion. I understood her fear. My mother had already "disgraced" her by having me out of wedlock for a ne'er-do-well of a steelband player. Moreover, a Methodist scholarship was paying for my school tuition and books. From New York my mother sent the money to cover the cost of room and board at the hostel where I stayed during the week. That night Vera Buchanan was present in the Hillsdale Circle, enthusiastically shouting amen. Reverend Johnston, our minister, had excommunicated her two months earlier because she'd let Lumley put her on mourning ground. She was a civil servant and had been our circuit steward. It rankled. I'd heard an angry Reverend Johnston discussing her conversion with Grama. After failing to persuade her to return to Methodism, he'd pounded the pulpit one Sunday, declared that she had "joined the Devil's band," and for that reason he was "casting her out from our fellowship. Sisters and Brothers, please pray that she will come to her senses and emerge from this heathen darkness and re-enter the communion of Christ." It probably riled him that he could no longer make her lose her job. In my mother's youth, Vera wouldn't have been so lucky. My mother had lost her teaching position because she had me out of wedlock, and for the same reason Grama had resigned her position as president of the Women's League.

Pointer Lumley's praying ended and Mother Biddy began to sing, "Come Ye that Love the Lord." Now audience and Believers clapped and swayed to the rhythm. As the Believers got to the refrain, "We are marching to Zion / Beautiful, beautiful Zion . . ." their eyes began to glaze over and lose focus, their bodies swayed independent of their wills, and sounds of shee, shee sheee, as though they were shivering, came from them faster and faster. And the first the signals of "journeying" sounded: *Hekay! Hekay! Hekay.* They had begun to "voyage" (*Pointer Lumley refused to tell me where*). People pressed in on one another, to witness the action. Mother Biddy began to jump—a mystery to me, how she did it. Summervillites said that under the influence of the spirit pain disappeared.

Now they were in high gear. *Hekay-hekay-hekay*, chorused the women. *Bouma-bouma-bouma-boum-boum*, replied the men, their feet thudding in perfect synchrony. All the Believers were jumping now. The singing stopped and there were foot thuds.

Hekay-hekay-hekay!

Bouma-bouma-boum-boum!

In the artificial light, they looked like leaping white gargantuan lilies. In the Ashby Circle, Sister Chloe, Mother Biddy's half-sister, stood out with an elephantine presence. "All the flesh her sister didn't get she took." Under her loose white frock, her large breasts, like pendulous gourds, bounced up and down, bringing her dress to her chin with every leap. After a ritual like tonight's, Summervillites—the teasing men mostly—would comment, "Man, did you see the action in Sister Chloe breasts? Is fourteen pickney she give birth to and every one o' them live." And in truth that was a rarity then among the Isabellan poor.

The jumping continued but now *Si ki yo ma sin pula micha hi sim lo hun ki lomi myoko lim* replaced the hekays and the bouma-bouma boums-boums. (*Jim, that's when we exit time and space and rediscover our Africanness.*)

Someone in the crowd began to sing "Work on believers like a light." The spirit caught a lanky fellow in the crowd and pulled him in among the Believers. "Hup-hup-hup-hup," he chanted and jumped. Sometime down the road there would be a rejoicing for him. And so it continued until they wound down. *Pointer Lumley refused to tell me how they knew when it was time to stop and what made them stop.*

Mother Biddy began to sing the soulful hymn "God Moves in a Mysterious Way," and everyone joined in. By the time it was over the Believers' eyes were back in focus and the circles around the leaders were restored, with a blindfolded Sister Aggie and Mother Biddy at the dead centre.

Now came the moment everyone had been waiting for.

Mother Biddy began to speak. Except for the breeze rattling the leaves of the nearby trees and the distant sound of the waterfall, there was silence. Even the village dogs chose not to bark.

"Sisters and brothers, we is always pleased to be in your presence. We thank the great God almighty for carrying Sister Aggie to the other side of Jordan and bringing her back to us in the land o' the living. You all know, brothers and sisters, 'The water is chilly and the river is cold'"—

"'It chill the body but never the soul," Believers and audience responded.

"Amen!" Pointer Lumley and Bishop Breeder intoned.

"Thank you, brothers and sisters, thank you. Tonight is Sister Aggie night. Tonight Sister Aggie come back to us full o' the light o' revelations. She come back purged of all evil. She come back full o' prophecy. She come back jam-pack with happiness and joy."

There were pockets of whispering. Her statements contradicted the rumours about her.

"As you all know, Sister Aggie is one o' we. She is a branch from the African tree."

"With strong-strong Carib roots," a male voice shouted."

The crowd applauded.

"True. True. Thank, you, Brother thank you. As you know, brothers and sisters, the spirit can call us any time, whether we is rich, whether we is poor, whether we is Dives or whether we is Lazarus, whether we is sick or whether we is well; and woe to the man, woe to the woman, woe to the child, who disobey. You all know what happen to Jonah"—

"Jonah went down to Nineveh, Nineveh," Bishop Breeder began to sing. We joined in.

After three verses, Mother Biddy raised her hand and we fell silent. Now she began to speak in an excited voice, like the prayer but without the amens. "Friends, when you make the journey/ to the other side,/ to the land of the shadow of death/ and see all the loved ones gone before/ friends, brothers, sisters, I can't tell you/ you must make it yourself/ you must walk the lonesome valley/ you must walk it for yourself/ Nobody else can walk it for you/ you must walk it for yourself/ and see" (*each see emphasized with a forward thrust of arms, head and torso*) ". . . and see . . . and see—yes SEE—all our loved ones happy, happy in Paradise"—her voice crescendoed, she closed her eyes and shook her fists—"Brothers and Sisters, when you make the journey/ and come back, YOU KNOW YOU DONE MAKE YOUR PEACE WITH YOURSELF, YOUR NEIGHBOURS AND GOD ALMIGHTY."

There was thunderous applause and foot-stomping.

In a calm voice she said, "Now friends, time to listen to Sister Aggie." She made a parting gesture with her arms. It meant that a clear passage was to be made for Sister Aggie, who was still blind-folded, for her to walk back and forth as she recounted her journey and her prophecies, and delivered the messages the departed had sent for their still living relatives. Mother Biddy walked towards the space she wanted cleared, and the crowd parted like the Red Sea under Aaron's rod. She walked back to the centre, to Sister Aggie, and held her hand to guide her, but Sister Aggie did not move. Mother Biddy pulled at her. Aggie did not budge. At first the audience and Believers were eerily silent, now a light buzzing started and quickly intensified. Aggie remained rooted like a megalith.

The cleared space closed in as people elbowed and pushed to see more clearly. They were moving into hallowed space. "Keep back!" Pointer Lumley shouted thunderously. Bishop Breeder unsheathed his wooden sword and brandished it. The bodies moved back.

"Cut her arse," a voice distinctly said.

"This getting hot," someone else said.

The Believers whispered to one another. Some gestured to others across from them. All solemnity was gone.

The opinions came loud and fast.

"Beat her!"

"I say confession good for the soul."

"Lance that abscess."

At this point Sister Beryl entered the centre of the circle and handed Mother Biddy a coil. Mother Biddy unwound it—a tamarind whip—pulled the blindfold from Aggie's face and let it fall to the ground. She lifted the whip to bring it down on Aggie's back, but Pointer Lumley grabbed her hand and shook his head.

The crowd cursed and hissed. There was a commotion then, and Bozo entered the circle, and he and Pointer Lumley lifted a catatonic Aggie out.

For months people talked about it. Most considered what Pointer Lumley had done to be sacrilegious. Mother Biddy later said she'd told Aggie not to have a rejoicing, but Aggie had demanded that she be taken to the Common and be beaten. The villagers prodded Mother Biddy to say what abomination had blocked Aggie, but to her credit, she never said. Perhaps Aggie never told her. Perhaps there was no abomination.

And so it was that Aunt Aggie lost her sanity that night, forty-seven years ago. A week later she was admitted to the Good Shepherd Mental Asylum. Pointer Lumley's intervention to prevent the beating created a schism among the Believers. Surprisingly, most of the followers went with him, and today it's his version, Reformed Believers, that is established all over Isabella Island. He dropped the African. A few Whites and half-Whites, admittedly poor ones, and a much larger percentage of the middle class now belong to the religion. And on Isabella Island and in Central America the mainline churches no longer excommunicate those who undertake *Dügu*. I don't know if Pointer Lumley got any more visions for Grama, because I went away to university, and when I came back I met her in an advanced state of dementia, and Pointer Lumley had died.

And I sit here now on Hopkins Beach, forty-seven years later, obsessed with finding out all I can about the Garifuna. Mr Coley has just told me that the living must make amends for the failings of the dead. And I wonder if Grama, a lifelong victim of anti-African propaganda, has been invisibly leading me to discover *Garifunaduáu* and to make amends for her failings. I have taken lots of photographs and made a video recording for my mother—now eighty-four. She too developed an interest in the Garifuna, even took a course on Garifuna culture at Medgar Evers College, and she has been attending the ceremonies that the Garifuna of Central America and the United States hold in St Vincent to commemorate the fifty percent of their number who perished in captivity when the British expelled their forebears to Honduras in 1797.

And Aunt Aggie? I am convinced now more than ever that some uncontrollable inner force made her enter that nether world where she'd hoped to reconnect with her Kalinago roots— perform as it were her version of a *Dügü*. But something went wrong, and she remained trapped in a state of trance. Perhaps she was fated to go insane, and the ritual merely triggered it. Perhaps I too will have to perform a *Dügü* and speak to her directly. *Dangerous undertaking, Jim. Could cost you your sanity.* I'll think on it further when I return to Montreal.

When the Bottom Falls Out

THEY ARE NOW SIX. Rob stares at the new cellmate, newly awak-
ened and rubbing his eyes, and probably wondering where he is.
He'd stumbled when the police unlocked the handcuffs and shoved
him into the cell about three hours earlier. He promptly stretched
out his skeletal frame on the floor as much as he was able to and
promptly fell asleep. He's too tall for the length of the cell and has
to bend his knees. His jeans are stiff with dirt, and the front of his
grey shirt is splotched with dried blood. He stinks—is probably
a vagrant— looks fifty or sixty, white but quite likely mixed, has
grime on his face and a three-inch slanted wound on his forehead.
The lips of the wound are bubbly, like caviar, and the blood has clot-
ted a dark red. His eyes are bloodshot, but even in the dim light Rob
can see that they are grey. Now those eyes are squinting and focused
on Rob. *Couldn't they have at least bandaged his head? That wound
should be sutured.*

"Hey, I know you," the man says.

Rob says nothing.

"All Isabella Island knows you."

Rob remains silent.

"How come you didn't get bail? Your boyfriend did."

Rob doesn't respond.

"Look, I ain't got nothing against your type, and don't you go getting all huffy with me 'cause you is a school teacher and I is a drunk. We's all in jail, ain't we? It don't matter who we was or is. I tell a policeman that was bothering me to go fuck his mother." He laughs. "And the son of a whore buss me head, buss me head and handcuff me and bring me in here. This world build on pure injustice." The prisoners listen attentively. With the exception of Fyfe, they all came to the holding pen after Rob.

"What's your name?" Fyfe asks the new man.

"My mother calls me Simon. But everybody calls me Doggie, and I prefer that. Look at me forehead. Ain't you see they treat me worse than a dog? And you is?"

Fyfe states his name and the other cellmates do likewise. Rob is the last in line, but doesn't have a chance to say it because Doggie says he already knows, and reiterates that everybody the length and breadth of Isabella Island does too. "Most o' the pictures only show your face, but in a couple you and your boyfriend are naked." Rob knows all this: for the sixteen days he has been here, he has had similar encounters with each new accused brought to the holding pen.

"So his papa didn't put up bail for you, eh. Now ain't that a bitch?" Doggie continues. "White people. Whaddya know! My Papa a white man too. Poor-trash white. Drunkard like me."

Rob wants him to stop talking. He wishes Fyfe would shut him up. Yesterday he'd shut up the fellow—he left this morning—who kept asking Rob how he could ignore "all that sweetness in pussy and turn to bulling. Disgusting. Man, you ain't know what you missing." He'd gone on and on for a close to an hour until Fyfe told him,

"Looks like you want to find out if it's really sweet behind there," and pointed to the fellow's bottom. The fellow—he'd refused to tell them his name—rushed Fyfe, who immobilized one of his arms and twisted the other behind his back and kept upping the ante until the fellow promised to calm down. "Now shut to fuck up before I get one of these fellows here to bull you till your arse busts." Fyfe winked at the other cellmates. The fellow began to tremble. Rob was grateful but fearful that he might have just contracted a debt to which he hadn't consented.

A police officer comes to the cell door, puts the key in, and beckons to Rob. "Looks like you getting off without any charges," he says and shakes his head in protest. "Times really changed. Bastard spent sixteen days dawdling and came up with this nonsense. Always making us look like jackasses. Everybody knows the law is ten years for bulling. What other evidence that fool wants?" He sucks his teeth. The officer takes him to the shower block, unlocks it, and hands him a shopping bag with clean clothes: a pair of jeans, a green short-sleeve shirt, socks, underpants, and a pair of sneakers, not the clothes he'd taken off the night just before the arrest. His mother must have brought them. It means that she knows he's about to be released. Who else knows? He puts the clothes on the cement bench outside the shower stall.

He takes off the orange overalls, showers and dresses, sits on the cement seat, and awaits the officer's return. *Looks like you getting off without any charges.* It's the most hopeful news he has had in sixteen days. Bail was set at $50,000 for each of them. Not a problem for Henry. He's a Colchester, from a family of ex-plantocrats, now proprietors of hotels and supermarkets. Henry left the holding pen the next day and said he would arrange bail for him. And that's the last Rob has heard. He'd thought that whatever hostility the Colchesters might have felt against him, they'd have at least done the necessary to get him out of custody. Moreover, he thinks Henry could have come up with the money on his own. *Left me in the lurch.*

He shakes his head and purses his lips as he recalls a comment from his days in Montreal. One Saturday he'd gone with a group of four gay guys—all undergrads at Concordia University—a Korean, a Nepalese, an Afro-Guyanese, and a Nigerian, to a gay club, and some nondescript white man had told him at least three times, "*Hostie, t'aimes faire suer des Blancs.*"[1] The first time the fellow said it, Rob thought he'd said *sucer*[2] and had replied no. *Now who causes whom to sweat?* Those four years he was indifferent to all the white men who tried to pick him up. The ease, promiscuity, and banality of gay sex there had struck him as undignified and not worth engaging in. When he told his friends he was returning to Isabella Island, they were taken aback. They'd assumed that the violence gays faced in Jamaica was prevalent in the other islands too. Eke wrote for *The Concordian*, and one of his pieces covered Peter Tatchell's work to ban homophobic dancehall singers from performing in Britain. "You are going back to the Caribbean!" Eke said, shaking his head in disbelief. Eke had already applied for refugee status in Canada. What Rob did not tell Eke was that he had a teaching job waiting for him in Isabella Island and that his mother had mortgaged her house to pay for his university education. His goal was to get to work as quickly as possible and start paying off the mortgage. *The right decision at that time. From afar evil always seems less frightful.* He sighs.

"Count yourself lucky," Edward, one of his cellmates, who'd been picked up in a ganja bust, said. "They found you naked but alive. Man, that's more than something to sneeze at." He was referring to a case, cold now for a few years—no suspects had been charged— of a man said to have been gay whose naked corpse had been found in

1 "Fuck, you like to make white people sweat."
2 suck

his car. "You guys couldn't find a more convenient place to fuck?" Edward continued. "Say praise God, we live in Isabella Island and not Jamaica." For sixteen days Rob listened to variations on this. Most times it was hard to sift out the sympathetic from the condescending and the hostile. Some comments began sounding like one and ended up being another. He understands. The subtle and unsubtle ways in which groups of people establish their pecking order is a phenomenon that has amused him since childhood. Even if he hadn't paid attention to any of this, one of his professors, as part of a lecture on the dynamics of human interaction, had made them watch the film *Glengarry Glen Ross* and asked them to write a two-page account of the struggle for alpha status among the film's four main characters. A lot of the male students had left class depressed that day. The staged humiliation the Isabellan police force had subjected him and Henry to, was that too related to alphaism? At the very least there was no physical violence against them at the site or here. There would have been if the media hadn't been present. In their adolescence most of those police officers would have thrown stones at persons identified as gay, or at the very least stoned their houses. At a Christmas dinner at his maternal grandparents' house, his cousin Murray had regaled them with a story about two bullermen he and some friends had caught in the bushes somewhere and pelted with stones. Rob looked at his mother and his aunt, expecting them to reprimand Murray, but the conversation had already turned to another topic. Here in prison, the abuse has been verbal, and all things considered, gentle. Fyfe's presence and empathy kept a cap on it. He remembers the prisoners killed in Jamaica, ostensibly because they were gay, without the police intervening. Nothing of this sort here.

And he owes it to Fyfe. A St Lucian. He'd been arrested picking up sacks of ganja left on the beach at Benoit's Point, a desolate and deserted part of Isabella Island that's accessible only by boat. Fyfe was taken into custody five days before Henry and Rob. Bail had been set at a million dollars. Rob suspects that when Fyfe isn't transporting ganja he spends his time at the gym. He's about six-feet—about two inches taller than Rob—but is at least one hundred and forty kilos of compact muscle. The guy's upper arm is bigger than some people's thighs. Rob sighs. *Yes, be grateful for small mercies.* Fyfe has been on his side, and now the charges have been dropped.

Now the challenge is: how to face the public and stare it down? What to say to relatives who'll accuse him of disgracing them? Will he still have a job? Probably not. Will he be able to find one? Two years ago, the most gripping part of the debate for a new constitution for Isabella Island centred on what rights should be given to same-sex persons. The resounding answer from every quarter except the anemic human rights group was, none. Joseph Glasgow, the chairman of the constitution revision committee—a former attorney general who'd resigned his office in exchange for the dropping of corruption charges against him—had with foaming-at-the-mouth rage informed an Isabellan television reporter that he would "never support rights for the likes of those. I want government in their bedrooms, under their beds, and in their closets: wherever they practise their iniquitous perversions. Above everything else, I don't want them in our schools. I don't want them luring my daughters into lesbianism and my sons into bulling." The reporter winced. Later, a columnist known for his humour had titled his commentary, "Looks Like Glassy Wants Them Dead."

Rob wonders if his mother shares those views. Last year, exactly two years after he came back from Canada, she asked him what was the status of his relationship with Elsa. She too had finished—a degree in French—and was teaching in Trinidad. "Hope you're not letting that girl slip through your fingers. You will look long and hard and never find another one like her." He'd dated Elsa for a little more than a year. She was twenty-one and he twenty-two when they began dating. They'd met at St Ignatius Secondary School—a Catholic school for boys staffed primarily by Christian Brothers from Canada—where they were both teachers. They hadn't yet gone to university and were exploring the feasibility of doing so. It was Elsa who'd figured out his sexual orientation—she never told him how, just that her gaydar never failed her—and taken the initiative and asked him to be her decoy. He'd seen the relief in his mother's face when he first took Elsa to the house. Linda was bubbly and overexcited all that evening. She's a Catholic who would walk on her hands and knees if the pope told her to. She's convinced that he's infallible. One time she told Elsa in Rob's presence that she looked forward to the day when she'd be her daughter-in-law. He thinks that her wish was less for Elsa's personality and more because she's Catholic. Elsa left to study at Catholic University in Washington, DC the same time he began at Concordia. The Catholic Church awarded her a tuition and board-and-lodging bursary on the condition that upon the completion of her degree she return to work at a Catholic school in the Caribbean. Rob wasn't so lucky. Linda had to mortgage the house to raise the money for his studies. His father, who'd been a law clerk, died when Rob was sixteen. He left them a mortgage-free house—thanks to an insurance policy—and nothing else.

What's taking the police officer so long? How's he going to face society now? His colleagues? Will he still have his job at St Ignatius? *Not a chance. The parents will want him gone.* The picture in *The Informer* showed Henry and him lying naked on the ground with a pixelated shadow at the groin. The shadow amused the cellmate who gave him the information. The piece in *The Isabellan*, his cellmate said, ended with the sentence, "Sex in an SUV should now be an example of unsafe sex." Rob shuts his eyes tight as he relives the beams of the police flashlights on him from all sides. The onrush of the media pack. Isabellan TV cameras and beaming light focused on them. He didn't count the bodies, but there had to be at least twenty. He and Henry tried to put on their clothes. At gunpoint they were ordered to leave them there, come out of the SUV, and lie supine on the asphalt of the Colibri Nature Reserve parking lot.

He and Henry had begun feeling each other out the last three months before Rob left for Concordia. It was Elsa who'd brought them together. Rob spent all three months vacillating. There were his Catholic teachings, the fear of scandal, Henry's womanish look and antics, and certainly their racial and class differences. Henry lived in his parents' house, located on two acres of land at Paradise Beach. From the beach it looked like an exquisitely kept park, with scattered trees and beds of flowers—floral islands in a green sea. They'd erected the property fence six feet from the water, ruining the natural beauty of the beach. Barbed wire topped the wall enclosing the property, and fierce dogs barked at the bathers on the public portion of the beach. Henry's one of about a hundred and fifty Whites of plantocrat descent still living on Isabella Island. He's five years older than Rob and teaches at Hanovertown Secondary. He has a master's in geography. Rob at times wonders why Henry opted to teach. Two generations ago, this would have been unthinkable; and arresting him, whatever the cause, would have been unimaginable.

Henry's gender-ambiguous look was problematic. It wouldn't have bothered Rob if they were living in Canada. His top-heavy torso and arms swing to one side and his hips to the other when he walks. His thick blond curls, pink full-moon face, porcelain-blue eyes, curved breasts from excess body fat, meaty hips, and soprano voice accentuate his womanly look. Isabellans always assume that gender-ambiguous men are gay and persecute them—although, even now, after fifty-two years of independence, class and race shield Henry: no one would dare to call him names, pick fights with him or stone him from a distance. And there will always be "a person is known by the company he keeps" mentality for Rob to deal with. The venom Isabellans suppress when dealing with Henry, they'd release with scalding furor onto him. Rob's neighbour Estelle—she's a widow—sometimes tells her three adolescent sons, "Know who can kick you with impunity and keep out of their way." It makes Linda cringe. Rob took every precaution not to be seen alone with Henry anywhere. Those three months before he and Elsa went off to university, she let him and Henry meet at her mother's house, always on a Wednesday while her mother, a teacher too, was attending meetings of the Marian League. There was never any question of taking Henry home or going to Henry's home. The subject never once came up.

When Rob came back from Montreal, he did not attempt to reunite with Henry. He no longer had Elsa's place where they could meet, and he wouldn't have felt comfortable going to the homes of any of Henry's friends. Then he assumed that Henry had friends. Now he's not so sure. After three months of putting Henry off— Henry had been calling him at home, a couple of time at St Ignatius too, until Rob asked him not to—Rob succumbed and accepted to meet him secretly, always at night. Wearing one of his mother's wigs, Rob would wait for him at the entrance to the Hanovertown cemetery. Thus began the night drives, on average once every two weeks, to the parking lot of the Colibri Nature Reserve. On the return trip Rob insisted on being dropped off at the cemetery gate, where he put on his wig and walked the three kilometres to his home on Mount Olivet. For almost a year that bucket went to the well. Sixteen days ago the bottom fell out.

Why didn't Henry arrange bail for me? "I have the feeling you are ashamed to be seen with me," he told Rob once and waited for a response. Rob was tempted to tell him the truth. Perhaps he should have. He wouldn't be in this sorry state now. Instead he denied it and said that since Henry wasn't associated with a girlfriend, if people saw them together, they'd conclude that they were lovers. Of course, Henry was very much aware of his own gender ambiguity. He told Rob that once his father told him that if he hadn't seen his willy as a baby, he'd be sure he was a girl. Henry's body is hairless and he can't grow a decent beard. His father lamented that. His parents had taken him to the United States for hormone tests and to inquire if his physiology could be altered. "Rob, they made me feel like a freak." He wiped his eyes. "When we got back to Isabella Island, I told my father I wanted a sex change. He said he would disown me." Yes, he sees clearly now. Refusing to be seen in public with him—he has added that to the list of humiliations he has had to endure. Why didn't he stay on in Britain? He'd done his degrees at London University and met his first boyfriend there. You would think he'd flee his parents' home the first opportunity he got. Maybe he would now.

Rob comes back to the moment. He hopes his mother didn't save the cuttings for him. He'll prefer not to see them. Worse, he hopes that down the road she will not use them in the guilt he's sure she'll saddle him with. It must be hard for her though. She spent every dollar she'd accumulated ensuring that he got the education he wanted. And until sixteen days ago she was very proud of him. When she came to see him three days after the arrest, the first time they gave her permission—she'd come directly from work still wearing her nurse's uniform—she said the court had refused her house as collateral because it was overleveraged and not much equity remained in it. She'd appealed to her brother Alban, a midlevel civil servant, to help her raise the bail money, but he said he hadn't that sort of money. Most likely true: he has a bevy of women, owns a BMW, and lives in a rented posh apartment.

Rob puts his hands under his chin and stares at the cement floor. Will his mother lose the house? He has no job to go to now. That's an absolute certainty. Will he able to find another? Could he return to Canada? How's the mortgage going to be paid? The arrangement with the bank had been to pay only the interest until Rob began to work. While he was at university he avoided asking Linda for anything. All four years—in winter, fall and spring—he wore the winter coat his uncle had given him. Alban had acquired it while doing a diploma in public administration in Toronto, and he'd kept it in case he had to travel to somewhere cold in the future. There were all the things Linda had deprived herself of in order to be there for him. When Aunt Margaret died in Antigua, she didn't go to the funeral. She never told Rob why, but he knew it was because she couldn't afford the trip. It was that or paying the interest on the mortgage loan. Margaret was her only sister and they had been close.

The officer returns, unlocks the gate and lets Rob out. Rob follows him into the office. The sergeant at the desk looks at Rob and grins—a grin to make you clench your teeth—the one you imagine on Dracula's face before he sinks his fangs into his prey. "Sign these," he says and pushes out a set of forms. Rob signs them and remains standing at the counter.

"What you waiting for? You is a free man?"

"My personal effects."

The sergeant picks up a phone. "Garry, bring the stuff we keeping for the bullerman—Robert Reynolds."

Rob caresses his chin with his left hand and stares at the counter. He waits for about five minutes before he hears the other officer's voice. The sergeant reads out the list of items: a wallet, a wrist watch, a cellphone, a gold chain, a set of keys. Rob sees them in the zipped plastic bag.

"My clothes?"

"What clothes?"

He hesitates. "The clothes your colleagues . . . "

"I'm not following you."

"The night. The clothes. . ."

"Oh, you mean *those* clothes." He chuckles. "I don't know where they is, nuh. I think they keeping them in case they have do a further investigation. I don't know. Check back in two days." He has a loud intake of breath followed by a pause. "You know what, man: go out by the back gate." He picks up the phone again. "Garry, come to the front desk. I go let Garry open the gate to the back and let you go out there. Boy, them media people out there waiting to take a strip off you."

Garry comes and the sergeant reaches under the counter and hands him a six-inch key.

Garry takes the key. "What's this for?" He waves the key angrily.

The sergeant's making hand-and-head don't-annoy-me gestures. "Let him out the back gate. That's an *order*, Garry."

When Rob's on the street, he takes his cellphone from the plastic bag. It's off. He turns it on holding his breath; there's enough power for a phone call. He phones Linda. She's at the front of the police headquarters. He tells her to stay there for the moment and he'll call her later. He walks four blocks in the direction of Mount Olivet. He boards the first bus that comes. It's a two-kilometre ride. As he gets off the bus, he sees the journalists, their cameras and microphones ready. He slithers away and walks quickly downhill to Nennie Beatrice, his godmother and a distant cousin, who lives about 200 metres down the hill. He knocks on her door frantically. She comes holding a pot spoon. She tears her eyes wide, opens the door, pulls him into the house, leads him to an armchair, and motions him to sit.

"What happen, Rob? You break outta prison?"

He shakes his head, and only then realizes how breathless and frightened he is. "The DPP decided not to lay any charges, but the media are outside police headquarters and in front of our house."

She takes his arm and leads him into the kitchen. "They treat you good?"

"Yes. Not a helluva lot to eat but otherwise okay." No need to tell her about all those bodies crowded together in a small cell. He sits at the kitchen table. A fatigue descends upon him that he's never thought possible. He slept in small patches while in prison: too many snores, no place to lie down properly. You slept sitting down on a stink blanket on the bare concrete. "Nennie Beatrice, can I go inside and lie down?"

She comes away from the stove, leads him into her bedroom, pulls back the bedspread and lowers the blinds. "When you get a chance, please call Mama on her cell and tell her I'm here, but not to let the media know."

She leaves. He gets into the bed.

Five minutes later she comes back with a pitcher and a glass on a tray. "Drink this." She puts the tray on the night table and pours from the pitcher into the glass."

"What's in it?"

"Milk, ovaltine, and rum. It will relax you and help you fall asleep."

He gets up, sits on the side of the bed, drinks a first glass and then a second before lying down again.

She leaves.

He thinks he'll be able to sleep now: a long sleep. Let the future wait.

Jen and Edwin

JEN WALKS TO THE WINDOW and looks out over Kingstown. She still has to get used to this new vista. Now that the house has a second floor, she's able to take in parts of Sion Hill and a larger part of Cane Garden. She was five when Aunt Milly bought this piece of land. Later, when Aunt Milly began building the first house—two rooms of cement blocks in the centre of the plot, so that "I can add on to it, if God spare my life and I prosper"—she told Jen that she'd wanted to buy further down but couldn't afford it, and that this piece, at the top of the hill and accessible only by a track, did not interest most buyers, and so she'd got it at a good price. At the time she and Aunt Milly lived in a rented room in Bottom Town.

Aunt Milly would be gone all day to sell in the market; and when the school day ended, Jen would walk to the market and remain there sitting on a crate and listening to the buyers haggle with Aunt Milly over the prices of vegetables. On Sundays after church, Aunt Milly got one of the taxi drivers to take her to various places—Evesham, Gomea, Vermont—to buy from the wholesale vendors. She especially checked the plantains and avocados for quality. She was proud of her reputation. Once she'd got two cartons of avocados that were beautiful outside but ropy on the inside, and some customers had complained, and it had bothered her to the point of offering to refund them. Some Sundays she took Jen with her, but most times after they'd each had a plate of delicious pelau, she'd take her to Higginson Street and let her stay with Ma Staples, Aunt Milly's class leader in the Methodist Church.

It's the 16th of July 2010. Thank God she does not have to teach. June was a disaster. Luckily her students were writing exams. She would have liked to be the one correcting them. She knows their weaknesses and strengths and would have been able to bring a more nuanced approach to the grades they got. She swallows.

Jen had lived with her mother Molly until she was two, and then her mother had "turned her life around," put Jen in the care of Aunt Milly, and left for Canada. That's what Aunt Milly told her when she was five. Aunt Milly never said what Molly had turned around from, and it's unlikely now that she would ever tell her. Until three weeks ago, when she met Edwin's father, she'd imagined all sorts of scenarios about the life her mother had led.

There are photos of Molly. Jen's favourite is one in which her mother is dressed in jeans and a yellow tank top. She's wearing humungous sunglasses with plenty of attitude, and her full lips are rouged strawberry red. Her arms are thin, sticklike, and her waist is narrow, wasplike. Something in her pose—the angle at which her head is cocked and her right arm akimbo—made Jen think Molly could take on the whole world. In the photo Molly's hair comes down to her shoulders and is wavy like white people's. Jen used to think it was a wig, because Aunt Milly has short hair that she braids in canerows, but after Molly died—Jen was thirteen then and in form two at Girls' High School—Aunt Milly told her it wasn't, that Molly's father was the son of the white man in whose house Audrey their mother had been a servant. Aunt Milly said she remembered when Molly was born. Audrey was thirty-seven then, and Aunt Milly was twenty. It was Aunt Milly who'd fetched the midwife. "Child, your mother was like my own child. No wonder I treat you as if you is my grand." The photos of Molly used to be in an envelope kept along with other knickknacks in a steamer trunk. Jen has since put them in a photo album.

It's these images that she used to hold in her imagination whenever she spoke to Molly over the phone. She and Aunt Milly would go to Ma Staples's home—usually on a Saturday evening, Christmas Eve, or the evening of Jen's birthday. Her mother always said how much she longed to see Jen, but Aunt Milly said Molly couldn't come back to St Vincent before she got her papers straightened out.

At first Jen couldn't understand why it was so difficult to straighten out papers, until Aunt Milly explained that when Molly arrived in Canada, the government had given her the right to stay for six months, but she had remained in Canada for much longer than that, and now she had to hide from the police until a lawyer could see the government and persuade it to let Molly remain in Canada for the rest of her life. From ages six to thirteen Jen wondered why the lawyer had taken so long. Aunt Milly said that maybe things moved more slowly in Canada than in St Vincent, but that in any event everything was in the hands of the Lord, and if the Lord wanted Molly to get her stay she would get it, and if the Lord didn't want it she wouldn't. The Lord knows best. And then the phone call came, and after that the newscast on NBC radio that Jen, her classmates—all Vincentians—heard: "A Vincentian, Molly Matthews originally from Rose Place, was shot dead yesterday in Montreal in what the police are calling a gangland slaying."

For a long time after, Aunt Milly became very silent. Jen was afraid to ask her if the Lord had anything to do with it. And the questioning might have made her sadder, and she didn't want to see Aunt Milly sad. Sometimes she would put extra food on Jen's plate and look at her as if to say, poor child, and sometimes she'd mutter, "God never gives us more than we can bear." And sometimes she'd sing "Must Jesus bear the cross alone and all the world go free. No, there's a cross for everyone and there's a cross for me." And when she got to, "The consecrated cross I'll bear till death shall set me free and then go home a crown to wear, a crown of victory," a peace would come over her, her eyes would light up, and she would smile. Whenever Aunt Milly sang that hymn, Jen would know she was dealing with some sort of inner turmoil, and it was amazing to see how calm the singing made her, as if it gave her some secret, comforting message—or calming mysterious medicine. She sang it one day at the market, after a woman, a relative, had come to quarrel with her for cutting her ties with them. She'd turned her back to the woman and stayed silent until the woman left. *I should sing it for her when I visit her this afternoon. Wonder if she'll hear me.* At home that evening, Jen asked about those relatives, and Aunt Milly said they weren't worth knowing. Jen pressed her: "Why?"

"Sometimes, child, it better to let sleeping dogs lie. When something dead, don't you bury it?"

Jen nodded, unwillingly. She didn't want to give up talking about it. Did she have cousins and great-aunts and uncles? She wanted to get to know them.

"Good. Well, that story dead, and I done bury it. No more questions."

Every year Aunt Milly and Jen went the last week in October to weed Audrey's grave, and on the night of November 1, All Saints Night, they covered it with lighted candles. She told Jen that the doctor said Audrey had died from an oversized heart, and she was sure grief had caused it. "Anyhow, she is in that place now, where there is no more sorrow, no more weeping, no more pain." She would begin singing the hymn then and Jen would join in: "On that bright, resurrection morning/ When souls and bodies meet again/ No more sorrow /No more weeping/ No more pain." And sometimes they would both begin to laugh, and Aunt Milly would pull her close and embrace her, and mutter, "God is good. He don't give us more than we can bear." She told Jen that Audrey, Jen, and she had lived together in the room in Bottom Town, but Audrey died before Jen was three, so that was why Jen did not remember her.

When Molly died they'd just moved into the little cement house, and it was a much longer walk to Ma Staples, who was by then feeble, and had a servant doing the cooking and cleaning. As much as possible, after Molly's death, Jen kept to herself. She avoided getting in her classmates' way so she wouldn't be told, "Your mother was this or mother was that." She'd heard them doing it over and over with other classmates, and she felt certain that behind her back they whispered.

By the time she wrote A-levels, Aunt Milly had added another three rooms to the house—a kitchen, a bathroom and another bedroom that became Jen's. At the market she now had a second stall and a helper who worked with her on Fridays and Saturdays.

It was around this time that Jen met Edwin. She was hoping to become a Spanish teacher, and he wanted to become a historian. He lived in Questelles, and sometimes she'd walk with him to the Leeward Bus Terminal and wait there with him until his bus came. Their relationship frightened Aunt Milly. "Hope you not doing nothing with that boy. Girl, listen to me good. Don't go out there and get pickney and throw way your future. Your mother did start out good-good, pupil teacher, and everything . . ." She stopped, swallowed loud, and became tense. "Just don't let that boy ruin your future."

She passed her A-levels with A-s. Edwin managed an A in history and Bs in his other subjects. She was awarded a scholarship and went off to Barbados to pursue a BEd. He stayed on in St Vincent and began to work in the civil service. They kept in touch by phone and by letters.

Her classmates at Cave Hill saw her as one of the lucky ones, for even before she'd finished at Cave Hill she was offered a teaching position at Carapan Secondary. Edwin was elated and insisted that he had been saving himself for her—whatever that meant—and they should get married. He said too that his father, who had been living in England and who only remembered him at Christmas, had come home to retire, and that they had become close. While in Barbados she was noncommittal, but when she returned to St Vincent and saw how gentle and thoughtful he was, traits she hadn't paid attention to before, she agreed. It didn't matter that she was taller than he, and he was stocky. If there were other women, she would have known. Vincentian women do battle to hold on to good men—and sometimes worthless ones.

She arrived home to find that Aunt Milly had added a second storey to the house and removed some of the walls on the first floor to enlarge the living room and create a bigger kitchen and dining room. Now the bedrooms were all upstairs. Aunt Milly had told her she was improving the house but hadn't said in what way. She no longer sold at the market. She'd rented commercial space on Back Street, and along with the usual fruits and vegetables, she'd added the usual imported staples—English potatoes, rice, flour, sugar, salted codfish, etc.—and now had two employees. Upon seeing Aunt Milly for the first time in four years, Jen realized that her aunt was tired. Her once firm, meaty body was sagging in places, the flesh on her arms jiggled, and there were pouches under her eyes. Jen wondered about the wisdom of enlarging the house. Whenever there was a drought—and those were becoming frequent in the Southern

Caribbean—hardly any water came out of the pipes. At 4 AM Aunt Milly would be up filling pails and pots, for by 6 AM nothing came out of the taps. There was also that steep hill to consider, especially for an older person, and the track was still the only way of accessing their house. During the rainy season it was muddy and slippery.

A week after she came home she asked Aunt Milly when last she'd seen a doctor. "What you asking me about doctor for? I don't need to see no doctor. When the good Lord is good and ready for me, let him come and take me. After I take you to live with me, all I prayed for was to live long enough to see you grow up and head in a path different from your mother. I say praise God, I done do that. You has a job now and a good education. I wish your mother was alive. She would'o been proud of you." Her face relaxed into a peaceful smile.

"Aunt Milly, what did my mother turn her life around from?"

Her aunt stared at the floor, said nothing for a long while. "Child, why you want to bring up old story? Your mother dead and gone. I sure she at peace where she is. Don't trouble yourself over what done happen. You can't change it. What you have to do is, 'Sow good seeds to everybody. Sow good seeds wherever you go. Over rocks and mountains, over hills and valleys, wherever you go, you must sow good seeds.' That, my dear child, is what you must do. The good Lord will take care o' the rest."

Had things gone as planned, she would have been busy all this month. They'd tentatively planned the wedding for August, a little too soon she'd felt, but Edwin had insisted. Guess he wanted them to be under the same roof, and he didn't have a roof of his own. He lived with his mother and knew that such a thing as living with her common-law in Aunt Milly's house was unthinkable, never mind doable. Jen has met Grace, Edwin's mother, several times. Aunt Milly has too, and it was when she found out that Grace too was

Methodist and belonged to the Women's League, that she'd begun softening a little towards Edwin. In her letters to Jen she'd mention that Edwin had dropped by her market stall, that Grace had brought her a sack of golden apples, that they'd met at a church rally and sat at the same table . . . Aunt Milly would have never mentioned them if she'd been uncomfortable with them.

When she told Aunt Milly that Edwin wanted her to marry him, she nodded. "That boy not stupid. He recognize quality when he see it. Marry him, but no make him load you down with pickney. The man-them does start out good-good and before you can say good morning Master Charley, them change and have other woman. But I like the young man. He got good manners, and I like his pedigree; he come from simple, decent people, like you and me." Jen's plan was to live on at Aunt Milly's after marriage, lead a Spartan life, and eke out the money to pay for Edwin's studies. He's passionate about history and would like to get a degree in it. She'd make it possible for him to go to Cave Hill and get it.

By then she'd felt free to begin having sex with Edwin—in his mother's house, of course, and taking care not to get pregnant. Aunt Milly's views on such matters were old fashioned. The affection! The thrills! So good she couldn't understand why she hadn't begun before.

It occurred to her then that she'd never known Aunt Milly to have a man. Why had she deprived herself of something so wonderful? It wasn't fair. She broached the subject gingerly. "You ever had a boy-friend, Aunt Milly?"

"Lots. Plenty boyfriends."

"That was before you took me to live with you."

"Child, why you want to get into my business? Ain't I did the best I can to raise you? Did I bring any worthless man in here to molest you when I turn my back? What foolish question you's asking me?"

112

"I'm sorry, Aunt Milly."

She was standing at the kitchen sink. Jen was sitting at the kitchen table. She came over to Jen and gently put a hand on her shoulder. She smiled and Jen was glad to see she wasn't angry. "Child, you have a good education, and you is pretty. Your mother, as you can see in the pictures, was a pretty woman. It get her into plenty trouble too. You have her beauty along with a good education. You can have your pick of men." She pulled out the chair beside Jen and sat on it. "At your age I been just a poor gal, and the men-them who used to come nosing around wanted one thing, and one thing only, and I saw what that thing left my mother with—two children she couldn't feed and shame, shame so deep, she carry it to her grave. I know she slept with Molly father to keep her job. She told me so. He didn't care what happened to her, so he didn't wear no protection. The result was Molly, and when Ma told the master and mistress who Molly father was, they fired her. Child, your mother was conceived in sorrow. She left here to get away from sorrow, and in Montreal she landed straight into the lap of sorrow. What can I say? I don't judge her. The Lord knows best. We will understand it by and by." She turned her head away and was silent for a few seconds.

"To come back to your question. I'm not saying that if a man I liked did come and offer marriage I would o' refuse. But the men who used to come around didn't know the first word 'bout responsibility. Sex, nothing but sex, that was all they wanted—same like now; most o' them would o' have to borrow the bed to do it in or would o' haul me into some dark banana field if I did let them. And after they done do that to me, how I could o' ever expect them to respect me? Vincentian women don't use their brains, Jen. They don't. And on top on that, Jen, them fellows depended on the pittance their mothers and sisters worked for. Child, God give us eyes to see with, and if we play blind we have nobody but weselves to blame. Sometimes I does sit here and wonder about your mother—if things would o' turn out differently if we did have a proper, responsible father. You didn' have no father neither. Molly refuse to tell us who your father is. But now that is not important. Not important at all. The danger is past. I thank God that you turn out all right. Now I can walk the streets o' Kingstown with my head high and go to my grave in peace."

Jen reached over and embraced her aunt. In that moment she felt it was no longer necessary to know the details of what Molly had done or for that matter who her father was.

The phone is ringing. She picks up the receiver. It's Myrtle, who lives in the house at the bottom of the hill. The postman refuses to come up the hill and leaves the mail there. She walks down the hill to Myrtle's house. She does so in dread. They told her she'd get the results somewhere around the first week of July. Today's July 16.

"How's your Aunt Milly?" Myrtle asks as she steps onto the porch holding three letters.

"Still in the coma. The doctors don't think she'll come out of it." Jen takes the letters from Myrtle, sees the name of the laboratory, and feels her heart begin to thump. She leaves quickly before Myrtle begins to ask her questions about the name on the lab envelope: Molly Cruikshank. Edwin had used an alias as well. They'd requested that the result be sent c/o Aunt Milly's address. She and Edwin had decided not to have the blood samples taken in St Vincent. The personnel there would have had access to the results. Anonymity would have been impossible. Somebody always knew somebody who knew somebody. The lab technicians would have been at school with Edwin or were members of their churches or had brothers or sisters or cousins who were their colleagues or in-laws. They'd found the lab via internet, made the appointment, flown to

Barbados one morning, given the blood samples, and flown back to St Vincent in the late afternoon. It had seemed so simple. Her only fear was that Aunt Milly might be the one to collect the mail on the day the results came. But fate took care of that.

At the top of the hill she's panting. Normally she walks up it easily. She goes into the dining room and puts the letter down. She remembers their promise to open it together.

That Sunday. Just over a month ago. Edwin had been bugging her to meet his daddy. She knew he hadn't been much of a daddy—he'd only sought out Edwin after he returned from England eighteen months earlier, and he never supported Edwin in any meaningful way while he was growing up. She didn't understand what all the fuss was about. After all she didn't know who her daddy was. The most she knew was that somewhere on one of the plantations, her grandfather lived or had lived. But which plantation, she knew better than to ask Aunt Milly. Anyhow Edwin said he couldn't put it off any longer, that his father really wanted to meet her. Not to have gone would have seemed awkward: the invitations to their wedding were already printed, the only thing remaining was to put them in the envelopes and mail them off. She'd told Aunt Milly about going to Georgetown to meet Edwin's father, Bertram Cruikshank. Aunt Milly reflected for a while, mentioned that she knew some Cruikshanks but didn't think any of them was called Bertram. She seemed indifferent. Fathers wasn't a topic Aunt Milly cared to speak about.

That Sunday she and Edwin headed to Georgetown in his cousin's car. She met, Annette, the father's wife, as well—a corpulent woman of South Asian and African descent. Annette was guarded at first. She brought out first a tray of sandwiches and one of cake afterwards. Bertram was African diluted with European, visible mostly in his hair. He ate nothing but quaffed several shots of rum. At the beginning he teased Jen. "Hope you ain't give me son nothing to drink to tie him to you. Never can tell with women. They love a man and they do anything to hold on to him."

"Dad, that foolishness died out with your parents' generation."

"You think so, huh. Anyhow I have to admit you snag a pretty one. If I wasn't so advanced in age I might o' been tempted to give you a little competition."

And the interaction might have continued and ended like that, if the wife hadn't asked "So who is your mother, Jen?"

"Molly Matthews."

Annette's eyebrows went half-way up her forehead and her eyes got small. "You heard that, Bert?"

He obviously had, for his hand shook and he spilled some of his rum. He downed what remained in the glass. "How old you is, Jen?"

"Twenty-three."

"Jesus Christ!" Annette said.

Jen looked at Edwin. Edwin's gaze alternated between his father and stepmother. Bertram's eyes were now fixed on Jen.

Edwin spoke then. "Will somebody tell me what's going on?"

Bertram leaned across to a side table and put down his glass. "Jen—I don't know how to say this, nuh. When you walked in here I say to myself this girl favour somebody I know. But I couldn't remember who. And now that I know who your mother is, it come back to me. Child, is my aunt you favour."

Annette interrupted. " Betram, why you don't just come out and tell the girl you is she father?"

"Father! Whose father?" Edwin asked.

"Hers. Jen. Who else? Jen is his child. A time Molly and me had *one* fight over Bertram. She pulled out a handful o' me hair and I sink me nails in her breast, and we tumble and roll and tear off one another clothes and hit and spit on one another until two women separate us. She been already pregnant with you. Then Molly went and get pregnant again. . ."

"That one wasn't for me. I didn' have no part in that one. Don't saddle me with that one," Bertram said, his arms raised defensively.

"And she go and abort it and the law catch she and she spend a year in jail. I already was in England when she get outta jail. Next I did hear she in Canada, and I know she wouldn't o' get to stay 'cause she did have a criminal record."

Jen sat rigidly on the sofa. Edwin was crying. Bertram was bug-eyed and alert. He spoke. "Before we jump to any conclusion lemme say this: other fellers' name got called with Molly. She was a wild one, a real good-time gal. Jen, is true that you resemble me auntie, but that might be coincidence. Let we not get carried away before we know more. Nowadays them can make test with DNA and them kind o' thing, and them can say for sure if you is my child."

Annette sucked her teeth and rolled her eyes. "See what all you alley cats does do? Look at the trouble you causing these young people now."

Bertram breathed loud but said nothing.

That was just over a month ago, but all that Jen remembers after the dismal news that Sunday was that she found herself in bed but couldn't remember how she got there. The next day she was weak with nausea and feared that she might be pregnant. Couldn't be. She was on the pill. The nausea continued and she got her doctor to give her a week of sick leave. In any event it was mid-June and the school year was almost over. On the Wednesday, seeing Jen's depression, Aunt Milly got alarmed. "Since you went out to Georgetown, you not the same. What happen? You find out up there that Edwin have another woman? . . . Why you in such a state? . . . Why the invitations still in the box?" Jen told her that she felt nervous about getting married. For one thing she had been thinking she would like to continue her studies, and she was encouraging Edwin to do the same thing. At that point she was only delaying the wedding, not cancelling it. "You not telling me the truth, Jen. Your voice don't sound like you is telling me the truth. You find out that he got another woman. I sure that is the reason. And I sure it got something to do with meeting that boy father."

"No, Aunt Milly. No. No." She shook her head vehemently. It was a good thing she didn't tell her the real reason because two days after this conversation, she found Aunt Milly sprawled on the bathroom floor. She would be in agony now and forever over whether the news had brought on Aunt Milly's stroke. She called an ambulance first, then Myrtle, who rushed up the hill to be with her.

After they returned from Georgetown, she didn't hear from Edwin for two days. She later learned that he too had taken time off from work. He came to see her on the Wednesday, right after her conversation with Aunt Milly. When Jen saw him coming up the path to the house, the roots of her hair began to tingle and she got goosebumps. Aunt Milly was inside the kitchen. Jen did not let him into the house. She didn't trust him to stand up under Aunt Milly's interrogation. She met him on the porch, took his arm, and began to walk down the hill toward the road. He suggested they begin the arrangements to do the DNA test. She agreed.

"Whatever the outcome, remember," he reminded her, "we're blameless in all this."

On the plane travelling back to St Vincent they agreed that they should open the envelope with the lab report together. In the meantime Bertram and Annette had promised not to spread the information. Edwin and she continue to visit each other. Edwin meets her at the house and they walk to the hospital together to visit Aunt Milly.

Once they went to the cinema together. To do otherwise would have aroused suspicion. St Vincent is small, and people are curious about their neighbours' business. In fact her colleagues—the fleeting moments in which she encounters them on the street, now that school's out—have been asking her if she is still planning to get married in August, and when she says no, she sees how electrified they become as they wait for gossip.

She picks up the telephone and calls him at the ministry of finance where he works. He says he'll come by in half an hour, his lunch hour. She goes upstairs so she can see him coming up the Kingstown Park Road and then up the track to the house. It's the longest half hour she's ever spent, and as it comes to an end, she is shaking.

A cab stops in front of Myrtle's house. It's he. She watches his short, squarish figure jogging up the track. She had found joy in that body, love in that man, had felt they were made for each other. *Let the result be negative.* She descends to the second floor to get to the door as soon as he arrives. He enters. She hands him the envelope. Still standing, he tears it open, his hands shaking. She watches the movement of his eyes reading the words. He drops the letter onto the floor. His arms fall listlessly to his sides, his face grimaces, and his eyes turn glassy. He moves to where she is and embraces her, and they both begin to sob.

Benita-the-Blessed

BENITA THE BLESSED. She wishes Cislyn would stop calling her that. *You can never tell with people. Can never know their real intentions. Sometimes I think she's mocking me.* The thought makes her uncomfortable. *No, not Cislyn.* Not her. Benita is lying on her back in bed reflecting on her recent trip to Jamaica: her first since she left fourteen years ago, and she wishes she hadn't gone. Then June was one and Bridget was three, and she'd left them in the care of her mother Hilda and had come to Montreal. Larry, the children's father, had promised to support them, and he did until he was gunned down four years later, when he tried to extend his *enterprise* beyond Savanna de la Mar into Negril. Hilda had known about his *enterprise* and had done everything to wrench Benita away from him. But Benita loved him, and moved in with him when Hilda's nagging became overbearing. In any event she was already pregnant with Bridget, and she didn't think she could take the daily barrage of accusations and insults that would come once Hilda found out.

She and Larry had lived together for three years, and he'd been a model boyfriend and father, *Nothing like those good-for-nothing Jamaican men that breed you and leave you and disown their children.* No, he wasn't like that, and she loved him for it. Now that Olivier has come into her life, she knows that Larry wasn't much of a lover. He got on top of her, did his thing, and rolled off. In Jamaica he was her first and only boyfriend, and she hadn't known that women were supposed to have orgasms and couldn't understand why she was always uptight after sex. Rafik, the Guyanese East Indian man she was briefly involved with here, was the same way: vup-vup sex and nothing more.

Sometimes she thinks she left Jamaica to get away from Larry. At other times she's less sure. He should have restricted his operation to the Savanna de la Mar area; he'd be still alive; should have learned from when he tried to extend to Kingston. From some of the talk she overheard between him and his operatives, the Kingston gang had tried to cut a deal with him, but he didn't take it. He must have felt that Savanna de la Mar was local, small change. He wanted his *enterprise* to be big, national. He was big-minded. She loved that about him. But that was trouble too. Those Kingston fellows didn't countenance people invading their turf. In fairness to him, he didn't involve her seriously in his *enterprise.* When he went off to collect or deliver supplies, he gave her specific instructions about what to do or say if anyone came calling. He was leery of people he didn't know but he always knew beforehand when the police were going to carry out a raid.

Then one night he invited her to accompany him to Kingston in his new SUV. He parked at Parade, rolled down the glass, and surveyed the scene. Then he got out, went to the back, took out a jute sack, and told her to wait inside. She was nervous. There was no one in sight. The street booths that hummed with sellers and shoppers during the day were all deserted. Kingston was not a safe place for a woman to be alone at night. She waited, locked inside the SUV for what seemed like an hour, but later when she heard the police report she knew it couldn't have been more than twenty minutes. Larry came back running, and then she heard the sirens coming from all directions. Soon the police headlights and torchlights were on them. He told her to tell them they had travelled from St Elizabeth.

A voice on a bullhorn blared at them to come out and put their hands up. They did as instructed. The officers approached and ordered them to put their hands behind their backs. They did so and the officers handcuffed them. She was grateful they didn't use their billy clubs on her or Larry. At the station they interrogated them separately. She told the interrogating officer, a half- Chinese man with glasses and a high-pitched voice, that she lived in St Elizabeth.

He laughed.

"Where in St Elizabeth?"

No names would come.

"Where in St Elizabeth?"

Afterwards she couldn't believe her mind could have gone blank like that—that she could become so confused.

"Mandeville," she blurted out, and right away knew she was wrong. Mandeville was in Manchester.

The officer guffawed.

"Why don't you just tell me the truth?"

At that point she had the presence of mind to stay silent.

Next there was all the tra-la-la of securing bail. Larry had no trouble coming up with the money to get her out of custody. The DPP looked at the evidence the police had collected against Larry and decided to drop all charges. But she wasn't so lucky. She never understood why they weren't dropped against her. Her lawyer—they paid him good money, some of it to buy off the judge—was confident that the case would be thrown out because the police officer had questioned her without informing her of her right to remain silent. Perhaps the judge had not been paid enough, all she knew was that she was found guilty of obstructing justice.

The lawyer wanted to appeal the verdict, but Larry couldn't come up with the fee. Besides, somebody with connections to the government had told Larry that the Americans were preparing to get nasty with Jamaica for not dealing with its drug lords. The pressure was on the judges to hand out a few convictions.

It rankled her that she went to jail and Larry got away. They released her from prison after seven months because of the baby she was carrying. She found out later that a police officer had warned Larry that if he insisted on extending his *enterprise* to Kingston they wouldn't be as "generous" next time. Larry too had pissed her off: *imagine him telling me, "I have business to attend to. Me is the bread winner and me have a whole heap o' matters to attend to: better you in there than me."* She couldn't believe he could think that, never mind say it, and she became convinced that he didn't come up with the appeal money because her conviction suited his plans.

When she left prison, she went back to her mother's house to give birth to June. Bridget had gone to live with Hilda while Benita was in jail. She also wanted to find a way to leave Larry. But that was harder than she'd first imagined. He loved his children and came once or twice each week to visit them. When he visited he always expected to have sex with her, and in spite of her resolve not to, she usually gave in.

And then her luck turned. Her friend Cislyn, who then worked in a hotel in Montego Bay, had met a vacationing couple from Westmount who wanted a nanny for their children. Cislyn offered herself, and they accepted and brought her to Canada. It turned out all right for her. *She is the one that is blessed, but from the way she groans sometimes, you will never think so.* She got her residency after two years, and to this day when various members of the Segal family are having parties, they hire her to help out with the preparations, and they invite her to their bar mitzvahs and weddings and treat her like one of the family. Benita and Cislyn corresponded regularly, and she begged Cislyn to find such a family for her. Cislyn found one that was prepared to hire her, provided she could get to Canada on her own. They couldn't be bothered with the paperwork and all that jazz. But Cislyn warned her that because of the jail conviction, she would probably never get permanent residency, and she should seriously consider that. Her mother always said where there was a will there was a way, and Benita found a way—or thought she did.

She looks at the clock: 10:50 PM Olivier is getting ready to leave work. He is the equipment maintenance man at a manufacturing plant all the way out in Pointe-aux-trembles. Cislyn thinks he's a great catch. Benita wouldn't go that far but accepts that he was a catch in the nick of time. Part of what Cislyn means, Benita supposes, when she calls her Benita-the-Blessed. From Olivier she has certainly learned the joys of sex. *That first time with him. Nibbling 'pon me ears, tickling me nipples, him tongue moving up from me knees till it hit the spot, and Lord when him lick me so, me could only grab the sides o' the bed and arch me body up and down like snake for no' bawl out, 'cause the next door neighbour would o' hear.* She'd vaguely heard that people did things like that—foreplay, that was what the woman on TV called it—but West Indians call it white people nastiness. She'd pulled away the first time Olivier pushed *cocky* in her face. She looks again at the clock over on the dressing table. He'll be here in forty-five minutes and will come into the bedroom and tickle her soles and run his hands gently up her thighs. She used to get wet just thinking about it. Not tonight.

Cislyn hasn't been lucky in love. The only fellow she ever stayed any time with, a Vincentian, had got her to empty her bank account on the pretext that he was going to set up a business, and then he took off and she never saw him again. *Imagine, taking all of that girl's life savings. I would o' hunt the bastard down and kill him. I don't know how she didn't go crazy. That girl went to school in the day and work in a nursing home at night until she get her diploma in nursing, and was saving up that money to buy a condo, and that scoundrel just come from wherever the wind blow him from and clean her out. I would o' kill him, as God is my witness, I would o' kill him.* Benita thinks Cislyn has soured on men since. A few of Olivier's friends would like to have a go at her. They ask Benita and Olivier to set them up. But Cislyn is indifferent.

"A friend in need is a friend indeed." Cislyn was a friend indeed. She's known her from the time Cislyn was five. Benita was six when her mother and stepfather and her sister Roberta moved to Savanna de la Mar. Cislyn was their next-door neighbour. In her memory there's still the image of the little half Indian girl in frilly frocks, her long hair worn in two side braids. Now Cislyn keeps her hair bobbed short. At age ten she began wearing glasses. A week after Benita moved to Savanna de la Mar, a hurricane blew the roof off Cislyn's house, and Cislyn, her two brothers, and their parents had slept on the floor of Benita's parents' house for two weeks until the roof was repaired. In 1988 Gilbert blew the roofs off both their houses, and they stayed almost three weeks in the Baptist Church. During that time her stepfather was in hospital with a broken clavicle from a beam that struck him on the shoulder. Hilda thinks he never fully recovered. He died three years later.

Her friendship with Cislyn makes Benita uncomfortable at times. Cislyn knows too much about her. One incident in particular. Cislyn was going on about Benita-the-Blessed, and Benita asked her, "How you so taken up with calling me that? Where you get it?" They'd run into each other in the food court at Alexis Nihon Plaza.

"You don't remember when I take you to meet the lady at the employment agency—the one that did get you your first sleep-in job in Westmount—you don't remember she did say that your name mean blessed?"

Benita didn't want to remember. It was right after she'd arrived only to find that the job she'd been promised had been given to someone else. Cislyn had taken her to this agency that placed domestic workers. It wasn't all that the woman had said out loud. The rest had made Benita very nervous. Cislyn heard it too, and Benita's hope that Cislyn told her the truth when she asked her if she had related her business to her friends. It won't matter now. Too late.

"Well, when I think of all the crosses and trials I done gone through"—she'd hesitated. She'd been on the verge saying it looks more like *cursed*. And then she saw why she'd hesitated. "Yes, blessed if you think of what I done gone through and I is still here."

Cislyn was insistent. "Look at it this way. I come here with me landed, and you come here illegal and stay illegal for twelve years— twelve years in which you never see the two gal pickney you leave back in Jamaica . . . "

Benita looked at her watch. She knew Cislyn was going to ask her about her daughters back home and tell her about her man troubles, and she didn't want to hear them. "Cislyn, I go catch up with you later, girl. I have to hurry home. A plumber coming to fix something in the bathroom." Of course there was no plumber coming to fix anything. Benita did not like to talk about her daughters back home. In fact, she was very uncomfortable with the name Benita. It wasn't the name in her passport. Moreover, whenever she could, she avoided places where Jamaicans gathered. But she couldn't avoid Cislyn, and she knew she had to treat Cislyn well because Cislyn knew her business. She hoped—dearly hoped to Almighty God— that Cislyn hadn't been publicizing it. Hilda used to say that "if you making poo-poo in the bush and you see a Jamaican coming, sit on it, 'cause they will go and tell the length and breadth o' Jamaica that they meet you making poo-poo in the bush." But Cislyn was the friend she came to, and all things considered Cislyn has treated her well. Once they had quarrelled, and she'd thought Cislyn would put immigration on her trail. But no, she hadn't done that. She knew so many people, who as soon as they quarrelled with the friends who had helped them, received a knock from immigration, were put in detention, and were deported shortly after.

In fact when immigration did come looking for Benita, Cislyn knew where she was, and didn't use her house phone to warn her. She used a payphone in the street. It was a complicated story. She was desperate and had latched on to Rafik because he had promised to help her straighten out her papers. He was Guyanese, forty-eight years old, eighteen years older than she. She'd suspected correctly that he had other women. One of them found out about her and reported her to immigration. Rafik had promised her that he would say he was her common-law spouse. The lawyer who was looking after her case—he'd charged her seven thousand dollars, and she had already paid him half—had given her the form for Rafik to fill out. He had also advised her at the very least to leave some of her clothes at Rafik's house just in case immigration sent someone there to investigate.

However it happened, one of his other women found out everything about her. Rafik must have told her. Some Caribbean men can't resist vaunting their virility—fantasizing was closer to the truth. They say that the more women they have, the more women flock to them. Apart from Cislyn, Rafik was the only person who could have known the telephone number at the TMR home where she worked then (she'd only lasted six months on the Westmount job.) He sometimes called her there. And how did his woman get Cislyn's address?

Half an hour after she'd fled her employer's house the immigration police showed up at Cislyn's place. *Well, I guess that is one way I am blest. I wasn't supposed to be still here in Canada.*

She'd phoned Cislyn from a coffee shop downtown, and Cislyn came and took her to stay with a Grenadian friend of hers. She'd begged Cislyn not to tell this friend her business, not even where she was from in Jamaica. The next week she went back to the placement agency, this time on her own, and the woman got her a job in another home. She told the woman, "I had to leave that job; wasn't anything I did wrong. Just that I had to leave. My boyfriend know I working there and he threaten to come there and kill me. I begging, you please not to tell Mrs Macmillan where I is." The woman frowned and Benita knew she didn't believe her.

For a while she'd got nervous about her status and even stopped communicating with the lawyer and Cislyn. Before the immigration incident she'd divided her days off between Rafik and Cislyn, now she stayed in her room. A little more than three months into the new job she ran into Cislyn one Sunday on the 124 bus. She'd vowed never to take it, but that Sunday she'd waited and waited for the Jean-Talon bus and had finally given in. Cislyn was on her way to Union United Church.

Cislyn had turned her head away and pouted when she saw her. Benita went up to her and said, "Good morning, Cislyn."

"Don't good morning me. You too damn ungrateful. Don't talk to me."

There was a vacant seat beside her, and Benita took it. After about ten minutes of silence, she asked Benita how things were and a conversation ensued. Benita explained that she was afraid the calls might be traced and that was why she hadn't called. That was in part true. Cislyn gave her a cellphone number and their contact was renewed.

That was nine years ago, and between that time and two years ago, during which Benita met and married Olivier, she had changed at least four employers—two she had quarrelled with, a third because the husband had come on to her, and the fourth because at first the woman seemed nice-nice and Benita begged her to sponsor her, and so the woman discovered that she was undocumented, and made her work for nothing on her days off, and began paying her twenty dollars less per week, saying that it was because the utility costs had gone up and she had to charge her more for room and board.

She comes back to the present, to her current dilemma, and doesn't see any blessing in it. Will her marriage survive? Olivier saw the change in her once she got back from Jamaica. His first statement after hugging her at the airport, was, "You look tired."

"I come down with food poisoning a few days before I left. I didn't tell you on the phone because I didn't want to alarm you." She'd come up with this explanation while on the plane, so that he would think that she needed time to recover, time for her nerves to settle.

She'd panicked when Olivier had proposed going to Jamaica with her. A good thing she was at the sink and he couldn't see her face. He wanted to meet her family, he said. He's puzzled that, apart from Cislyn, she has no friends. He's the opposite: a total extrovert with friends everywhere, in all classes and in all races. He loves to give parties, and to go to parties. There's hardly a Saturday night they aren't having one or going to one. She complains that their one-bedroom apartment is too small for the thirty-plus persons who come, but he ignores her. On party-giving Saturdays he wakes her up early, and together they head down to Plamondon to buy West Indian foods. Josephine, his Antiguan ex-wife, got him hooked on them, and he in turn got his Canadian friends hooked. When they return home, he gets out the two roasting pans—they are the only containers big enough to hold the meat they bring back: chopped up oxtail and goat—and they begin the cooking. She would have already baked cassava pone the day before. *That man loves cassava pone.* By then she would have put the breadfruits to roast in the oven and would be helping him to chop garlic and grind spices. While the pressure cookers hiss away, he washes and dries and puts away all the utensils they used. A neat man. One of the many things she loves about him. She told Cislyn about his many qualities, and hinted at the ecstasies in the bedroom. Undoubtedly what Cislyn was referring to yesterday when they talked on the phone, and she again called her Benita-the-Blessed.

She met him three years ago, at a bus-stop of all places. She'd noticed him ogling her. He wasn't the first to do it. There were always horrible looking white men propositioning black women all the time. She and Cislyn sometimes joked about it. Cislyn told her the stories other black women had told her. After chewing her up with his eyes, Olivier eventually introduced himself. At the time he was 38, three years older than her. He told her he'd been married to a woman from Antigua, a nurse, who'd left him. He said he'd supported her decision to take leave of absence from her job to upgrade her qualifications, and after she'd done so, she felt she was too good for him. Benita was sure it was more complex than that. He said he would like to take her out for coffee and get to know her better, and he gave her his telephone number.

She'd waited a week before calling him. Cislyn had told her she had nothing to lose. And indeed that was true. It was eleven years she'd been living undocumented here, and she was sure that one day her luck would run out. He took her to the cinema on Sundays. On occasion, they went for walks on Mount Royal. They'd been doing this for at least two months before he attempted to go to bed with her. He lived in a studio basement apartment on L'Acadie. The apartment was neat, everything in place. About ten months into the relationship she told him she was undocumented. He wanted to know how she could become documented, and she told him he could change her status by marrying her. Three weeks later they went to the court house and got married.

If she'd thought that Cislyn hadn't heard what the woman at the employment agency had said out loud, after the wedding, Benita couldn't doubt that Cislyn knew that she had come to Canada using her sister Roberta's identity. Roberta was the name mentioned when she took the marriage vow. She'd already told Olivier that Benita was a nickname she'd been given by her grandmother. At the restaurant later, where all of Olivier's friends were gathered to celebrate the occasion, Benita spent a great deal of time studying Cislyn's face for signs of alarm, but she saw none.

In the days following, she thought things through and decided that she should have a candid talk with Cislyn. She not only had to set the record straight about the name she was using, there was also the question of her daughters. She had to know whether Cislyn had told her business to anyone. Moreover, Cislyn would now be coming to their apartment, and Benita did not want her blurting out embarrassing information. A week after the wedding, she arranged to meet Cislyn on one of her days off. Benita offered to pay for the lunch, and Cislyn objected and advised her to spend her husband's money cautiously. Olivier had stopped Benita from working and told her to wait until she could do so legally. They went to a West Indian Restaurant in NDG, and from the time they got there until the main course came, neither said much to each other. Benita noted that Cislyn was looking at her warily. She recalled that when she'd told Cislyn that Olivier had offered to marry her, Cislyn had replied that she would sooner turn lesbian than marry a white man. "What you will do if your mother-in-law call you nigger?" But when Cislyn met Olivier, she admitted that "him look alright, "and after a pause added, "anyway you need him for get you outta the fix you in."

Benita picked up her knife and fork and saw that her hands were trembling. She saw too that Cislyn was staring at her hands.

"Why you so nervous?"

"Cislyn, you *know* why I nervous."

Cislyn too picked up her knife and fork and did not answer.

"Cislyn, you think I was right to come to Canada the way I come?"

Cislyn didn't answer. She continued to eat.

Benita waited a while. She'd put down the knife and fork. She hadn't yet touched her food.

"Cislyn, you didn't answer my question?"

"Benita, what you want me to tell you? I don't know. I did warn you 'bout that criminal record. Where your sister Roberta is now?"

"She living in Port Maria with her husband. He does go to the States every year to do farm work."

"They have children?"

Benita nodded and indicated three with her fingers.

Cislyn continued to eat. "Your food getting cold."

Benita suddenly felt nauseous and had to excuse herself to go to the bathroom. In there she vomited. Her stomach had felt nervous all morning, and all she'd had was a cup of ginger tea.

When Benita resumed her seat, Cislyn said, "Benita what bothering you? I know you invite me here to tell me something important. What is it? First, I did think you going to tell me you pregnant, but now I see is something else, something that troubling you . . ."

The hiccupping sobs came then. Cislyn went over to Benita and led her into the bathroom. When they came out, Cislyn told the waiter to pack their food and to call a taxi for them. The taxi soon came, and Cislyn gave the driver her address on Dupuis.

They got to the apartment and Cislyn made Benita a cup of ginger tea and gave her a gravol. "Now tell me what you have to tell me." She said, sitting across from Benita.

"Cislyn, when I filled out my application for residency I put down that I don't have no dependents, and I told Olivier that Bridget and June is my nieces. I tell him that I help my mother out with them because they is orphans."

Cislyn said nothing.

"Olivier don't have no children. His first wife was a career woman and didn't want children to hold she back. She studying for her master's in Ottawa. Maybe I should o' tell him the truth. He might o' like to adopt mines. What you think, Cislyn?"

Cislyn opened and closed her fists and stared at the floor and said nothing. She took off her glasses and wiped them with the tail of her blouse and put them back on. Finally she spoke.

"So you don't want me to ask you about your children when your husband is present? That is what I think you telling me. I get it. I won't ask you. I won't even ask you about your nieces. Did you notice: I never ask you about your sister? Never. After I heard the receptionist at that domestic workers' agency say out your name loud. She was questioning it. Doubting it. That is what she was doing. She probably knew that a lot of the girls don't use their real names."

"Cislyn, you think I should o' come here in my sister name?"

Cislyn frowned and shrugged.

"Well, I wasn't going to sacrifice my future 'cause of a stupid mistake I make in my youth."

Cislyn said nothing.

"Cislyn, I been thinking that when I get citizenship, I might have to leave Olivier. I hope to God he don't find out the truth before and leave me." She stared hard at Cislyn.

"Don't look at me like that. I don't go around prattling off my mouth."

"Cislyn, you tell anybody that I come to Canada in my sister's name?"

Cislyn didn't answer right away.

"Answer me. Lawd Jesus! Answer me, Cislyn."

Cislyn raised her arm, gesturing calm. "No, not directly, but I was at a party one time, and I met some people there who knew you or knew about you—they talked about the prison sentence in Jamaica—and they were wondering what your status in Canada was. One of them was an ex-girlfriend of Rafik. I don't know if she was the one that we think tried to get you deported."

"You mean they got people here that know me!"

"Lawd, child, stop your foolishness. You think you and me is the only Jamaicans that come here?

"You told them anything?"

Cislyn shook her head. "Nothing at all."

"Cislyn you think that that is a fair way to treat Olivier?"

"You mean lying to him?

Benita nodded.

"What you want me to tell you? I know I tell you I don't want no white man around me, but I think that if you go all the way and marry somebody you should be honest with them. That strike me as plain common sense. On top o' that Olivier married you to make your status regular. Otherwise is common-law he would o' propose. He already get burned in marriage once, and by a black woman too. You should o' been honest with him. I would o' told you so if you did ask me about it. Why you didn't ask me?"

"Don't know. Didn't think about it all. Cislyn, I want you to tell me if I was right to disown my daughters?"

Cislyn frowned, twisted her lips, spread her palms, and bent and straightened her fingers.

"Talk, Cislyn. Tell me what you think."

"I think you asking me to judge you. I can't do that. I ain't God. One thing I will tell you though: Olivier is doing right by you, and I don't think you should use him and then dump him."

"Cislyn what you think would happen if Roberta find out that is her name I used to come to here?"

"I don't know."

"When I did it she did done leave home and working as a maid in Mandeville."

"How you manage to get a passport in your sister's name? That piece puzzled me. Who sign your passport application?"

"I can't tell you. I swear to my cousin Bobby—you remember him?" Cislyn nodded.

"I swear to Bobby not to tell nobody. He tell me that if they find out what he did they would fire him from the police force. I tell him not to worry. I won't tell nobody."

"You just told me."

"I did?"

Cislyn chuckled. "Don't worry. I don't go around talking about things that don't concern me."

"Well, I might as well tell you. Was a lawyer that signed it, and I don't remember his name.

Cislyn shrugged.

Their conversation turned to other topics.

That encounter was two years ago, and since then Cislyn has been to many parties at her house, though she has never once invited Benita and Olivier to her place for supper. Benita wonders if it's because Olivier is white.

She gets up to go to the bathroom. Olivier should be home in about twenty-five minutes. He'd cooked so much food to welcome her back from Jamaica that they're still eating it. All she had to do this evening was to steam some vegetables. The fridge is crammed with left-over pork chops, roast lamb, jerk chicken, rice and peas . . . She thinks he forgot that he was cooking for two, or maybe he'd thought of inviting some of his buddies by but changed his mind. That's something she's going to have to try and change—*if I around to change it.* Too many bodies coming and going; too much socializing. Too much money spent on entertainment. She hopes he doesn't show up here one day with somebody who knew her in Savanna de la Mar.

She goes to sit on the couch in the living room, and her mind fixes on her recent trip to Jamaica. If she had met her children in the street, she wouldn't have known them. The last photos she had of them were from five years earlier. Cislyn had taken them on a trip back to Jamaica. So as not to leave traces for immigration to follow, Benita had prevented her family from writing to her. When she sent money it was always through Western Union. Wherever she worked she mentioned her two orphaned nieces who were in their grandmother's care, and her employers would give her clothing from friends and relatives to send to them. Clothing too for "the dear old lady." She sent home a barrel of clothes every year.

When Benita saw her mother seventeen days ago, she looked like seventy, and she told her that Bridget and June were unruly. "When it come to that cross, Bridget, is a sure sign that what in goat also in the kiddy. Don't think is trace I tracing you . . . You see she not here. You see. It going on midnight and she not here. She off gallivanting. The boy she fooling round—bitty, dung-gut, good-for-nothing, dwarf of a bwoy. Him strut like fowlcock. Hold him head like fowlcock too. Stand up in front o' my gate and word me off. The only thing that force-ripe man didn' call me was whore. Lemme ask you this, Benita: Is come you come carry them back with you? I hope to God that is so, because you is liable someday to hear I pick up something and lick down that wretch that you name Bridget. You see how all the trials and tribulations she done put me through leave me looking *obzacky.* And me feeling *obzacky* too. The doctor tell me I need tonic and me sugar high. Botheration cause it. That been me whole life: botheration. It start with your puppa, after that with you. Then you go out and breed, and you dump your pickney-them 'pon me, and it been botheration ever since. And what is the thanks I get? Once in a while you send me a pittance and some ol' clothes. You see the old board house me is in? Take a good look. Woodlice done gone through it. Roberta say she would o' help me with a new house, but since is your pickney-them what going live in it, it should be your responsibility."

Benita regretted then that she'd made the trip. On the phone, apart from asking her when she was coming to get her children, Hilda didn't tell her stuff like that. She left Hilda in the living room and went into the bedroom she was sharing with her, to get a reprieve from the lecture. She heard the door open. "Good night, Grama," she heard Bridget's voice.

Hilda stcupsed. "Don't good night me. Benita, you see the hour she coming home? You tell your mother everybody saying that you throw 'way pickney?"

"Grama, please don't start that again. That is why I come home late. I was hoping you already in bed. If my father didn' dead I would o' leave here long time and go live with him."

"Yes, and come drug pusher too."

That's my mother alright. A nagger.

"I hope is come your mother come to take you off my hands. I don't mind your sister, though one o' these days I will burst that lip o' hers. But you—I can't wait to get you outta my sight."

"Grama, you don't think you talk too much. Your mouth don't get tired? Mammy is so she used to carry on with you?"

Benita wanted to laugh. She agreed with Bridget, but she would have to take her mother's side. She went back into the living room then, and stared at Bridget standing half a metre in from the main door. In every way she looked like her father: smooth round face, flattish nose, big laughing eyes, tall lancelike body: almost two metres. June looked more like her: narrow face, aquiline nose, fleshy lips with slight buck teeth, large hips and buttocks. They both have that ripple in their buttocks that draws lewd comments from Jamaican men. When she first met Olivier, she wondered why he used to lag behind her, and when she turned to look at him, he'd be blushing and his eyes glowing; when she asked him why, he asked her to promise that she wouldn't get mad with him. She promised, and he told her it was because he admired the way her buttocks bounced when she walked. After that she always tried to make sure she was never ahead of him.

Around 3 PM the next day, Benita opened her pocket book to get some money for her mother, who was going grocery shopping, and saw right away that someone had rummaged through it. She looked closely and saw that an envelope into which she'd put five hundred American dollars was missing. She asked her mother if any strange person had visited. Hilda said no. "If you missing money, is nobody else but Bridget that thief it. I forget to tell you. I can't leave money nowhere where that thief can't find it. She too thief." Benita gave her mother the Jamaican dollars she'd gone looking for and sat down waiting for Bridget to come home.

Hilda returned from the grocery store and cooked and they ate. There was no Bridget. June said she was sure she was at Punta's place. Benita asked June to take her there. They walked down the street about three blocks and turned into a narrow alley. Another fifty or so metres and they were there.

They met Punta under a mango tree tending meat on an improvised barbecue: a half drum cut lengthwise. Booming reggae music came from inside Punta's shack. About a dozen young men and young women lay about cuddling, bottles of beer in their hands or on the ground beside them. The smell of ganja was thick. Benita looked at the smoke rising from the barbecue grill and thought, there go my American dollars.

Somebody must have seen them coming, because when June asked Punta where Bridget was, Punta grinned, waved the spatula he was holding, and said he didn't know anybody by that name. Then he shouted to the folks in the yard. "All you know any somebody what name Bridget?"

No one answered.

"See, Missus. I tell you we don' know nobody name Bridget."

"Man, stop playing the fool, Punta," June said. But Punta returned to tending his barbecue.

Benita felt like a fool. She swallowed her anger and told Punta, "Well, if anybody by that name smell your cooking and come by for some, tell her a woman named Benita wants to see her. She knows where that woman lives. Tell her too that it would be easier than if the police come."

For a few seconds Punta became rigid like a statue. Then he turned to face her. He shook his head. "Naw, Missus, you no go send for police, 'cause you went to Canada in your sister name, and all somebody have to do is report you to the Canadian government and is right back here your backside will end up."

His cronies chuckled. To this moment Benita does not understand how she managed to remain standing. On the way back to the house, she begged June not to tell her grandmother what she had heard.

Bridget did not come home that night. "See for yourself what I been trying for tell you?" Hilda said.

Bridget came back at midday the next day, stood outside the door, and said she had come for her things.

"You touch one piece o' them clothes and see I don' chop off your hand to rass. And you see her carrying on like this, the bwoy does slap she off good and proper in front o' people, call she slut and all kind o' names. Benita, I shame till. I shame. That is what you give birth to."

"Keep quiet, Grama. You always dribbling. Lemme get me things before I cause ruction. Mammy, I will write the Canadian government and tell them you come to Canada with a false passport, if you all don't let me get my stuff." She said it loud, most likely so the neighbours would hear.

"False passport! What kind o' false passport you talking 'bout, Bridget? You outta your head?"

"I telling you, Grama, that she—Mammy, Benita—she travel to Canada in Auntie Roberta name. That is what I telling you, Grama. That is the reason why she up there all these years and didn't send for me and June. She couldn't send for we, Grama, 'cause the name on we birth certificate don't match the one in her passport. That is what I telling you." She stared at Benita with a big grin. "I was only going to take one hundred dollars, but when I read what in your passport I take the whole envelope."

"Fire and brimstone!" Hilda said. "Benita you do that for true?"

Benita did not answer.

Bridget tried to move past Hilda who was standing on the porch. Hilda blocked her.

"Now if you will excuse me, move out my away. Lemme get my things."

"Shut up! You hear me! Just shut up. Right now." Hilda said. "You not leaving here to go live with that piece of shit that insult you coming and going and beat you up for sport. What he give you to drink that turn you dotish? And when he breed you and drop you—'cause, as God is in heaven, that is what going happen, soon as he find a woman to mind him—where you will go?"

Benita was too stunned to remember what happened next and, for that matter, the rest of the day. She didn't sleep all night. Bridget didn't come home that night.

Her ability to think came back the following morning. She still had eight days remaining in Jamaica. What would she do? Half of Savanna de la Mar would know in a week what she had done. There was the story that pretty well all Jamaica knew, of two sisters, identical twins, from Savanna de la Mar. A visiting American had married one, and taken her to the States. Later the other sister went. About fifteen years later both sisters were deported back to Jamaica. The married sister had let the other sister come to America with her documents, and when her marriage broke up, her husband denounced them, and they were deported.

That morning she stayed in bed long after Hilda. She didn't eat the breakfast which Hilda prepared. Around ten Hilda left for the doctor's. Benita saw her chance. She hurried out of bed, had a bath, threw some clothes in her carry-on luggage, and walked out to the street and boarded the first bus that came along. It was headed for Mandeville. In Mandeville, she took another bus and went to Montego Bay. There she spent seven days in a guest house and lived as if she were in a coma.

She was nervous as she went through Canadian immigration. The officers, both women, got suspicious and searched every crevice of her small luggage. It was while they were searching that she remembered that Olivier had asked her to bring back a couple bottles of Jamaican rum. It was only when she got to the arrivals area and saw Olivier waving to her, that a load left her shoulders briefly. That same night she dreamt that an immigration officer accompanied by Bridget had come to arrest her.

At some point she'll have to tell Olivier—it would be better if he hears it from her first—and accept the consequences, and it will have to be soon. She'll have to tell Cislyn too. She doesn't know what she will tell Roberta. *I can only hope that she will understand. Hope that she don't come with demands too. At least I didn't have to deal with her while in Jamaica.* There's no way she could go to immigration and recant her story. They'd say she got her residency fraudulently, arrest her on the spot, put her in detention, and deport her. She hears the key turning in the lock. She gets up from the couch and meets Olivier at the doorway.

Olivier

OLIVIER IS STRETCHED OUT ON the sofa in the living room. He's tired. He hasn't slept for more than a few hours in the last couple of days. Those phone calls. Benita is having an affair. How did it come to this? Deception. Again. He was up at four and drove all the way to St-Raymond-de-Portneuf to attend the ten o'clock funeral of his brother-in-law. He'd dropped dead of a heart attack on the job. Age 49. Probably while insulting an employee. Right after the interment, Olivier drove back to Montreal. Karine was miffed that he wasn't staying for the repast. "*Hostie! Tu ne restes pas! Merde! Olivier, tu es trop rancunier! C'est samedi. Rien ne presse.*"[1] she told him this as he held open the car door for Benita. He took a step towards Karine to embrace her, but she raised her arm defensively and went into the house. She's his older sister, and on issues that didn't involve her husband they've always got along well.

He'd gone to the funeral to offer her his support, not out of any

---

1 Goddamit! You're not staying for the wake! Shit! Olivier you're too spiteful. It's Saturday. What's the hurry?"

love for Serge. He had none. And he was sure that for him Serge felt something worse: contempt. Because Serge's old man swam in money, he felt he could spit on everybody. Serge's father owned the local sawmill. Olivier had gone to work there at eighteen. Serge was the hands-on manager. Vincent, his papa, preferred to stay in the office. Guess the buzzard had to make sure his office staff wasn't fleecing him. Serge had just married Karine after knocking her up. She was twenty-one and he was twenty-six. Whether or not Serge was pissed off about having to marry her and took it out on him, Olivier cannot tell. What he knows is that Serge rode him and humiliated him at every opportunity, and made him do the worst jobs: sweep up sawdust, clean the toilets, make coffee, going into St-Raymond to buy pastry for him. Serge called him every insulting name that came into his head : *débile, vaurien, crétin, couillon*[2]. The breaking point came one Monday morning when Serge told him, "*T'es pire qu'une tapette.*"[3] Olivier grabbed a two-by-four and let him have it. To this day he isn't sure where the blow landed, he doesn't remember anything else except that he had walked home, sat on the sofa in his parents' living room and waited for the police to come.

His mother was surprised to see him home at that hour. His father was home too. At fifty-one, he was on permanent disability. He had worked in Asbestos, and he smoked heavily. Half-way down the street you could hear his lungs rattling. The diagnosis was emphysema, made by the company's doctor, and was attributed to smoking. Of course it was mesothelioma, but that diagnosis was made three years later when his father was hospitalized, a mere two weeks before his death.

That morning his mother, Hyacinthe, pressed him for an explanation. He gave her none. She had begged Vincent to give him that

2 Cripple, stupid, cretin, jerk.
3 "You're worse than a faggot."

job. She did not work. His father's small disability pension was not enough to pay the bills. His sister Marie had moved to Quebec City the year before and was living with her boyfriend, and members of the family were under strict orders to say she was going to school there.

«*Qu'est-ce qu'il a fait?* »[4] He heard Hyacinthe say on the phone in the kitchen.

. . .

« *La police, monsieur!* »

. . .

«*Je vous en prie, Monsieur, n'appelez pas la police.* » [5]

There was at least five minutes of silence during which he wasn't sure if she'd hung up the phone, and then she said, «*Essayez, monsieur. S'il vous plaît, essayez. Il est jeune. Hâtif et impulsif. Donnez-lui une seconde chance.*" [6]

. . .

"*Merci, monsieur. Que Dieu vous bénisse, monsieur!*"[7]

Olivier heard the phone click and decided to bolt. He wasn't going to sit there and listen to his mother pour out her woes about how she had sacrificed herself for her children, about his father's ruined health, about her children's ingratitude, about the shame Marie had brought her. And he wouldn't have put it beyond her to accuse him of trying to break up his sister's marriage. It was a mild October day, and since he didn't know what else to do, he kept walking along Grand Rang, all the way to Pont Rouge. By then he was hungry and had no money on him. His mother had prepared a lunch for him but he'd left it at work. Lise, a girl he went to high school with and was in love with, worked at the IGA in Pont Rouge. He hoped she wasn't off

4 "What did he do?"
5 "I beg you, Sir, don't call the police."
6 "Try, Sir. Please. Try. He's young, hasty, and impulsive. Give him a second chance."
7 "Thank you, Sir. God bless you, Sir."

work. He went into the grocery store, hoping to see her. He didn't. A cashier told him she was on her lunch break, and asked if it was urgent. He thought for a while—yes, urgent for him, but he didn't think it would be for her. No, he told her. *"T'es certain?"*[8] He nodded. He told her he would come back in about forty-five minutes. As he left the store he saw his reflection in the glass and realized that he was in his work clothes and there was sawdust in his hair. No wonder the cashier had seemed so anxious. He returned and told Lise a bit of what happened, and Lise gave him ten dollars. He hitched a ride back home, and told his mother to leave him alone.

It wasn't until he was at Hyacinthe's funeral in 2001 that he thought about her intervention on his behalf. It saved him from getting a criminal record. He wouldn't have the job he has now. He'd had to sign a form authorizing the company to do a security clearance on him before they began training him for the job he now holds.

He's tired and hungry. He hears Benita knocking around pots and pans in the kitchen, and he smells chicken cooking. Maybe he should have grabbed something to eat at Karine's house. He couldn't. He'd vowed never to enter that house. Serge was dead, but it was still his house. Maybe if she'd had the reception at the hotel. It's where most people hold their funeral repasts. Guess she wanted every Pierre Jean-Jacques to see and feel envious of her home. No, he shouldn't think that of her. He understands her disappointment. She's a peacemaker. She'll get over it. She has come to his place many times, and she and Josephine got on very well; in fact they're still friends.

Josephine did not share his view of Serge, but Josephine comes from a privileged family and was blinded by the life of luxury Serge and Karine led. In the early years of their marriage Josephine talked

8 "Are you sure?"

breathlessly about Karine's jewellery, the furniture in their house, and whatnot, until Olivier told her he didn't want to hear about it. Once after she'd come back from visiting Karine and Serge—she always went alone, by bus from Montreal, and Karine picked her up at the bus station in Quebec City—she asked Olivier what a *plan nègre*[9] was. He asked her where she'd heard it. She replied that it didn't matter; she only wanted to know what it meant. He told her he'd never heard the expression before. She said then that Vincent had asked her if she knew what a plan nègre was.

"Why didn't you ask him to tell you?"

"I heard the word *nègre* and I was sure it had to be something bad about Black people."

"Could be." He hoped his voice and face weren't betraying him. She never asked him about it again. Deep down she might not have wanted to find out, fearing it would jeopardize the relationship she had built with Karine and her husband.

After the incident at the sawmill, he wasn't able to find a steady job in St-Raymond. For a few hours a couple of days he helped a charcoal burner chop wood. And when his uncle Jean-Marc, who was the gardener at Église St-Raymond, fell ill in mid-October, he got Olivier to rake the leaves and put the garden to bed at the presbytery and the church grounds. By mid-November there was nothing to do. If he'd had a car, he might have tried finding work in the surrounding communities. A recession was on, but he thinks it was more that the news of what he'd done had spread. Small towns. Can become prisons. He sighs. On his applications he left the space for work experience blank. One of the fellows who interviewed him for a job knew somehow that he'd worked at the sawmill and asked why he hadn't mentioned it. Olivier replied that it wasn't much of a job, that was why.

9 A nigger plan (any project that's doomed to fail).

On December 1, he withdrew the sixty dollars in his *Caisse popu-laire* account and went to Quebec City, where he found a job wash-ing dishes in a restaurant. During the three years he spent in Quebec City, he got a driving licence and took English classes at Université Laval. And then he moved to Montreal to have more opportunities to practise his English.

Benita comes to him from the kitchen. "Come put something in your stomach."

He gets up, goes into the kitchen, and sits at the table. She has pre-pared a bowl of stewed chicken, a platter of fried plantain, a bowl of plain rice, a bowl of cho-cho, carrots and string beans, and a pitcher of sorrel.

He continues his reverie while eating. He still cannot fully explain his attraction to black women. As a teenager in St-Raymond, he saw Aretha Franklin, Diana Ross, the Staples Sisters, Nathalie Cole, Tina Turner . . . on TV. Their looks didn't displease him but it was their music that he loved. Even then the only music he loved more than R&B was reggae. The rare occasion a car drove through St-Raymond with black people in it. But that was it. There was no one black at his school. One Chinese boy and a Vietnamese girl, that's all he remembers. He'd thought the girl, Lynne—he never knew the boy's name—was Chinese too until one day he heard her correcting a girl who'd asked her a question about China. Once he was sitting with some boys outside a restaurant, and Lynne walked by with a man who was probably her father, and one of the boys said that his mother had told him that when she was little everyone believed that Chinese people had sex with their noses. He chuckles and sees Ben-ita staring at him. Lynne got married to a cousin of the composer Luc Plamondon. She probably met him while she studied music with his aunt who was the organist at Église St Raymond for as long as Olivier could remember and long after he left.

On the Laval campus he saw many black women, blacker than the American stars he saw on TV, and he fantasized about what it would be like to play with their naked bodies. Their bulging buttocks fascinated him. For the first time he became conscious that his own were as flat as a kitchen counter, and whenever he saw Quebecois men with nice round buttocks, he always wondered why he wasn't one of them. When he moved to Montreal, he started training at a gym with one objective: to enlarge his gluteus maximus. His butt got firm alright but not a whit bigger.

In Quebec City he slept with a girl older than he who was a waitress in the restaurant where he worked. She was from Chicoutimi. She'd wanted them to move in together, but he wasn't passionate about her the way he had been about Lise. Lise never let him past her clothes. "*Le mariage d'abord. Ensuite le sexe. Pas avant!*"[10] —her blue-green eyes ready to taser him. She too came to Montreal and married a Japanese.

The phone's ringing. Benita gets up to answer it.

He expects to hear her say, "Sorry wrong number." It's what she says whenever the man calls and Olivier is home. Later he usually checks the phone memory and sees that it's the man's number.

"Hi, Cislyn. We is eating right now. I will call you back."

In Montreal he held all sorts of jobs until he got his break to learn machine maintenance, which he now does. His love of reggae brought him in touch with West Indians. There was a club on the Main where they played reggae music, and he went there on Saturday nights. Over time he got to know some of the regular patrons and got friendly with them. A few of them invited him to their homes and he appreciated it. Michael, Josephine's brother was one of them. He now lives in Calgary. That was how he met Josephine. She'd just finished her nursing program in Antigua and Michael

10 "Marriage first. Sex after. Not before."

had rewarded her with a trip.

He will never be able to say exactly what happened to him when he first saw her. He still remembers every detail: the pale beige blouse, the dungaree skirt that reached all the way down to her ankles. Her hair was in a brush cut. She wore hoop earrings of black coral. Her skin was obsidian, the colour of the African women he'd seen on the Laval campus. Her lips were two fleshy protruding petals. No lip gloss. They parted to show a gap in her upper incisors. And what a smile she had. It dimpled her cheeks. Her waist was narrow and her chest buxom. Her hips matched her chest: an hour-glass figure. His heart was already beating fast, but when she turned around and he saw her buttocks, he was certain everyone could hear his heart beat. He shoved his sweating hands into his pockets. She was a couple of inches taller than he. He said very little to anyone there that night. There were Michael and his brother Joseph—he was studying dentistry at McGill—and their girlfriends, and three other women, school friends of Josephine who had moved to Canada. He doesn't remember their names.

Michael had already told him that Josephine was returning to Antigua in ten days. When Michael followed him out to the elevator, Olivier took a deep breath and asked if Josephine had a boyfriend.

"You like you interested, man."

He nodded.

"You going have to ask her that yourself. Wait a minute." He went back inside the apartment and returned accompanied by Josephine and left her facing him alone.

After about a half minute of silence, she said, "So?"

He took a deep breath, then stumbled out the words, "You're beautiful."

She chuckled. "That's why you kept looking at me all night?"

He didn't know if he should answer that. He didn't think she had noticed.

He took the deepest breath he could manage and said, "I would like to go see a movie with you. That is if it won't cause any trouble."

"None at all."

They went out a few times, always inexpensive outings. In those days he hadn't much money. She wrote to him when she returned to Antigua, and then he did one of the stupidest things a person could do. He told his boss a sister had died and he needed a week of bereavement leave. He worked as a shipper for a clothing manufacturer then. He used up all the credit on his credit card, withdrew what he had in the bank, and made up the difference with half of his rent money, bought a plane ticket to Antigua without letting Josephine know he was coming. He settled in a cheap hotel in what he later learned is the Fort James area, and phoned her. Her mother answered the phone and said Josephine was on night duty. He left the number of the hotel and hung up quickly before she could question him.

They met the next day. She came to the hotel still wearing her work uniform. He'd wanted to know if there was anyone in her life. She told him no. When she took him home to meet her parents, and he saw the huge house they lived in, the maid and the gardener, he was sure she would not want to marry him. The dinner he had at her house the Sunday before he left! The silverware and expensive crockery! The maid bringing in the different courses and clearing out the plates they'd used. Her father was an MD and her mother a high school teacher. From the simple way their son Michael lived, in a roach-infested one-bedroom apartment on Goyer, Olivier would have never suspected he came from *la haute bourgeoisie*. He'd never asked Michael what he did. He wondered what the parents thought about the dingy hotel he was staying in; and what they would think, if they saw his mother's clapboard house, with bedrooms smaller than their clothes closets and leaning to one side because of its damaged foundation—the cellar flooded every few years, whenever the Saint Anne River rose above normal. He returned to Montreal discouraged and unprepared to deal with an irate landlord. Three weeks later, in addition to his fulltime job, he began working part time as a general helper in a restaurant, and after several months he cleared his debts.

Benita interrupts his reverie. She clears the table and asks, "You want a cup of tea? I didn't make any earlier because I thought you would o' want to have a nap seeing as how we got up so early."

"Yes, a cup of tea. You know if I sleep now I would lie awake all night."

For a little more than a year Josephine continued to write to him. He preferred to call. He didn't trust his written English, and he didn't want it to make an unfavourable impression on her. Then their correspondence lapsed. The offer to train for the machinery maintenance job came around that time. In the interim he'd met Rosita, a girl from Trinidad. They had lukewarm sex for about eight months. Maybe her beige complexion couldn't get his hormones going, but it was probably the long list of things she gave him of what West Indian women didn't do in bed. And then he found out that she had left behind four children in Trinidad that she wanted to bring here; and she asked him if he would be willing to be a father to them. She'd also lied to him about her age. She'd told him she was twenty-three, and she looked it too, but she was thirty-three, and her eldest, a boy, was sixteen. He was twenty-six at the time. He told her he wasn't ready for that kind of responsibility and left her.

What with working at the restaurant on weekends, he'd stopped going to the reggae club and lost contact with Michael. He'd also changed addresses and phone numbers. One Saturday morning about a year after he'd left Rosita he ran into Michael in the men's department at the Bay.

"Josephine and I talked about you last night."

"How's she?"

"Alright, but frustrated. Angry that she can only work on a temporary permit until she passes French."

"She's in Montreal?"

"Let me have your number. I'm sure she'll want to call you."

Three and a half years had gone by since they'd first met. She called and came to his studio apartment. They made love that same evening. He hadn't made love to her before. And yes her complexion did things to him. And she didn't have a list of thou-shalt-nots. They had been sleeping with each other for about seven months, when she proposed that they move in together. He balked. That would be too serious. She no longer mesmerized him, and he had images of the wealth he had seen in her parents' house, and was sure she'd have expectations he couldn't meet. She wanted, she said, an account of all the women he had been involved with after he came back from Antigua. That wasn't difficult. There had only been Rosita.

"It's your turn now," he told her. They were lying on his hide-a-bed.

She said nothing.

"You mean all this time there was *no one*?"

"There was someone," she said. "There was someone and he made a fool of me. That's why I'm in Canada."

She didn't tell him more that night. It came out in dribbles. His name was Perry, and he was a British doctor who'd specialized in tropical medicine. Marriage had not been her objective, having a good time was. They did lots of things together. Sometimes they took off to nearby islands for a weekend. Eight months into the relationship she discovered that she was pregnant. That was not supposed to happen. She'd insisted that he use condoms. He wanted her to keep the baby but wouldn't marry her. Just as she entered the third month, she made an appointment in the USVI and had the pregnancy terminated there. Two weeks later, she applied to immigrate to Canada.

"Now that you know my story, I hope you won't judge me."

"Not at all."

In the end it was he who proposed marriage. He wonders now if in his unconscious he'd felt that what she'd gone through had shaved away some of the inequality. She said she would accept but there was one condition: she hoped to go to university and get a degree in nursing, so she wouldn't want any children to distract her. He accepted and they got married. He helped her with her French and she passed the exam and got certification. Two years later, she entered McGill and did her degree. They lived in a one-bedroom apartment to keep the expenses down. He did pretty well all the domestic chores so she would have more time to study. When she got the degree—she was now twenty-eight and he was thirty-two—he told her they should start thinking of getting a house, and if they were going to have children they would have to do so now. She was non-committal about both. She said she'd got the learning bug and might want to continue studying. He lost his temper and they quarrelled. He'd done all he could to help her realize her dreams and he could see that her accomplishments were pushing them apart, that with each achievement she wanted something more. They promised to remain on friendly terms, and they have, sort of. They call each other on their birthdays and at Christmas and New Year's.

He's sitting alone at the table. He hears the sound of the television. Benita's in the living room watching it. He picks up the mug of tea. It's cold. He doesn't remember seeing when she put it on the table.

It's happening all over. Again. For the last couple of weeks while Benita was out, a man with a Jamaican accent—he thinks it's a Jamaican accent—has been calling the house and asking to speak to Benita. A few times too when they were both home, the phone rang and she'd hurried to answer it, said wrong number, and hung up. He has tried redialling the number but is told every time, "we do not accept calls at this number." The man must also be calling when he's not here. His impulsiveness, almost got him a criminal record at eighteen. He should have never married a woman he didn't know. He remembers now that she didn't want him to come with her to Jamaica. Is she hiding something? Since her return she's been claiming to be sick. How long does it take to get over food poisoning? Now when they're making love he can feel that she isn't there with him. Probably fantasizing about being with the man. He hardly slept last night. He has to find out who this man is. Why doesn't he leave his name? Why doesn't he leave a message?

"Benita," he calls quietly. "Come into the kitchen. There's something I want to talk over with you."

She comes and sits down across the table, facing him.

He breathes deeply. He hates confrontation. His stomach churns. At work he does the jobs of those under him rather than get into confrontations with them. He's fidgeting.

"What is it, Olivier?"

"A man . . . has been calling here for you and he doesn't leave a message. I think he has a Jamaican accent. In any case he has a Caribbean accent. Do you know who he is?"

She doesn't answer.

"I noticed too that there are times when the phone rings and you pick it up and put back down the receiver without saying anything more than 'hello' and 'wrong number.' Is that your code to tell him I'm home?"

She's frowning and holding her breath. She covers her face with her hands and she begins to sob.

"What's happening to you?"

She swallows a few times, waits for her sobs to settle, and then speaks. "My name is Benita."

"I know that. One of them anyways. It's the name you use."

"You don't understand. I am telling you my name is not Roberta. My name is Benita."

"Okay. So how's that related to the man who's calling here?"

"He calling to blackmail me 'cause he know my name not Roberta. Roberta is my sister name. I come to Canada with a passport in her name."

He's silent. Stunned. "Does your sister know?"

She nods. "Before, no. But now I sure she know."

"So why you came to Canada in your sister's name?"

She tells him the story about her involvement with Larry and her imprisonment, and explains that with a criminal record it would have been impossible to get residency status.

He feels the anger mounting. He gets up, walks to the living room and comes back. "So who's this man that's calling you?"

"He name Punta."

"How he found out? "

"She starts to sob again."

This time he doesn't feel sympathetic. He's annoyed. He walks again to the living room and comes back.

"Okay. What other secrets you have to tell me?"

She says nothing.

"DO YOU HAVE ANY MORE SECRETS TO TELL ME?"

She nods and holds her head down.

"Okay. Talk. Tell me."

"I have two children in Jamaica. Their father is the same man that cause me to go to jail. They gun him down nine years ago. Punta is Bridget boyfriend. She find out about the passport and tell him, and he tell everybody, and now he know he can use it to shake me down."

Hc sits down. IIe's cold. He feels the freeze in the tips of his fingers. *Tranquille. Tranquille. Tranquille. Calme-toi, Olivier.*[11] His mother's voice comes to him as it did in his childhood.

"I didn't want to deceive you, Olivier. I didn't want to. I was planning to tell you everything. But I was waiting till I get citizenship. I should o' never gone back to Jamaica. That was my big mistake."

"You have two daughters in Jamaica! What are you saying?"

And then he remembers *The Joy Luck Club* in which a woman said she left her two daughters on the road in order to save her own life. He'd told himself later that it was cinema, fiction, not real life. The war in Bosnia was going on when he saw that film. It was the first time he'd spent time reflecting on the cruel things humans do to one another. He returns to the issue at hand.

They sit in silence for a long time. It gets dark, and he gets up from the table and turns the light on. He walks over to the side of the table where she's sitting, puts an arm under hers. "You must be tired. Come, get some rest."

He gently leads her into the bedroom and seats her on the bed. He leaves, heads to the liquor cabinet, and pours himself a drink. He goes to the linen closet for a duvet and a pillow. He'll sleep on the sofa. Hopefully in the morning his head will clear and he will be able to think. He goes to the bathroom and brushes his teeth. He pauses at the bedroom door and listens for her breathing. He doesn't hear it. She's not asleep. He doesn't bother to go into the bedroom for his pyjamas. His underclothes will be enough. He stretches out on the sofa and hopes sleep comes. At one point he hears his mother's voice echoing in his head : «*Celui sans pêchés, c'est lui seul qui tienne le droit de lancer des pierres.*» [12] And he remembers that if Serge had pressed criminal charges, he wouldn't have the job he has

---

11 "Calm yourself. Calm yourself. Calm yourself, Olivier."
12 Only the sinless person has the right to stone sinners.

today. Worse yet if the blow had killed or maimed him. He goes to the bedroom. Benita's eyes are on him. He puts a hand on hers. "You made some foolish decisions, but I understand. I made some too in my youth but I was luckier than you. Try to get some sleep. Tomorrow we'll try to figure something out."

Acknowledgements

I wish to thank my publisher Nurjehan Aziz for supporting my creative endeavours and her contributions to Canada's multicultural literature; M G Vassanji for his astute editing; Rudolph Coleman and the wonderful residents of Hopkins Village, Belize for the inspiration that led to the writing of "Garifuna"; and the members of Ilona Martonfi's writing group who've offered valuable critiques of my work.

Some of these stories were previously published in slightly altered versions: "Guilty and Innocent" (with the title "Death of a Murderess"), in *Matatu;* "Glimpses into the Higginsons' Closet," in *Wadabagei;* "The Headmaster's Visit," in *Kola;* and "Emory," in *Beyond Sangre Grande: Caribbean Writing Today,* Ed. Cyril Dabydeen, 2011.

Nigel Thomas was born in St Vincent. He attended university in Montreal and for ten years was a teacher with the Protestant School Board of Greater Montreal, before joining the faculty at Laval University, Quebec, from where he recently retired. His published works include the novels *Behind the Face of Winter* and *Return to Arcadia,* and the short-story collection, *Lives, Whole and Otherwise.* He received the Homage to Artists award from Laval University in 2013.